Ghosts

of

Georgetown

Ghosts
of
Georgetown

——— . . . ———

ELIZABETH ROBERTSON HUNTSINGER

JOHN F. BLAIR, PUBLISHER   WINSTON-SALEM, NORTH CAROLINA

DESIGN BY DEBRA LONG HAMPTON

PRINTED AND BOUND BY R. R. DONNELLEY & SONS

Library of Congress Cataloging-in-Publication Data
Huntsinger, Elizabeth Robertson, 1958—
    Ghosts of Georgetown / by Elizabeth Robertson Huntsinger.
      p.   cm.
    ISBN 0-89587-122-X
    1. Ghosts—South Carolina—Georgetown County.
2. Haunted houses—South Carolina—Georgetown County.
3. Georgetown County (S.C.)—History.   I. Title.
GR110.S6H85   1995
398.2'09757'8905—dc20   94–46288

*This book is for
my parents and
my husband:*

Alasdair, Virginia, and Lee.

Contents

Acknowledgments

For their interest, time, help, and information I owe a debt of thanks to Bettye Marsh, Graham Reeves, John and Patricia Wylie, Mike Streppone, Hal Drotor, the late Robert Tucker, Todd Gwinn, Dr. Dwight Williams, Jane Ware, Buddy and Shirley Carter, Robert Mitchell, Joe Craven, Dr. Jim Michie, Capt. Sandy Vermont, Eileen Weaver, the staff of the Georgetown and Waccamaw Neck libraries, and my fellow members of the Huguenot Society of South Carolina.

For critical readings of the manuscript I am grateful to Carolyn Berry and Elaine Bestler.

For their energy and enthusiasm in guiding this book into finished form I owe a great debt of thanks to Carolyn Sakowski and Andrew Waters.

Prologue

Since the early eighteenth century, the port of Georgetown has been a busy center of trade for the South Carolina low country.

The history of Georgetown began in the early 1700s. Land grants in what is now Georgetown County were given to colonists by the British Crown as early as 1705.

By the early 1730's, the port community of Georgetown had been laid out in proper town lots and had become an official port of entry for the colony of South Carolina.

In the years that followed, great harvests of lumber and indigo floated through the fertile, green low country, down the Waccamaw, Black, Pee Dee, and Sampit rivers, to the burgeoning port town. Georgetown's location on Winyah

Bay, at the convergence of these four rivers, made it a commercial center for the entire area.

After long sea journeys, great tall-masted ships sailed into Winyah Bay and the port of Georgetown loaded with commercial goods from Europe. They left the port with their cargo holds full of the raw materials that were so abundant in the New World.

During the Revolutionary War, the British occupied Georgetown and used it as a base for their operations in the area.

After the war, Georgetown's economy flourished as rice, grown on local plantations, became the city's chief export. Rice plantations prospered along the rivers that meet at Georgetown. The North and South Santee rivers, which run into the Atlantic ten miles south of Winyah Bay and form the Santee Delta, were perfect areas for rice cultivation.

In the early 1800s, a lighthouse was strategically placed on the shore of Winyah Bay near the entrance to the city. The lighthouse improved navigation through the port, and caused another boom in trade. As the port of Georgetown flourished, the planters, whose exquisite homes graced the county's rivers, grew increasingly wealthy and influential.

However, Georgetown's antebellum way of life changed drastically after the Civil War. Stripped of their fortunes and vast labor force, many plantation owners were forced to give up rice planting, while others persevered in making a meager living from their fields. A series of hurricanes in the early 1900s permanently ended profitable rice planting in Georgetown County. The abandoned rice fields were left as lonely havens for waterfowl.

Fishing, shrimping, lumbering, and other non-agricultural ways of life began to replace the rice culture, and Georgetown remained an active port.

During Georgetown's history, many of the unique and colorful characters who lived in the area created lasting impressions on the town and the surrounding countryside. Some of these individuals left details of their lives carved in stone or written in historical volumes. Others, however, left impressions of a more ethereal nature.

Georgetown County is reputed to be one of the nation's most haunted places. There are rumored to be over a hundred known ghosts in the area.

Although many of these hauntings are suppressed by descendants or those concerned that a home's historical value will be overshadowed by a ghost, many Georgetown residents delight in describing the habits and background of their ghosts.

Ghosts do have habits. They repeat the same action over and over, and with few exceptions, are usually more predictable than frightening.

It is not known for certain why this county has so many hauntings, but several theories exist.

A place near the water which makes it prone to dampness is often more subject to spirit activity than drier areas. Not only is Georgetown County located next to the ocean, it is virtually filled with the waters of the rivers that flow through its moist and fertile lands.

In the last two-and-a-half centuries, many individuals have died suddenly and unexpectedly here. It is believed that such a death causes a certain amount of energy to remain in the vicinity where the spirit left the body.

Many believe the type of personality most apt to leave a deep, lasting, and distinct impression is that of a person who was obsessive or possessive. The immeasurably wealthy seventeenth- and eighteenth-century planters, and their progeny, were individuals known for extraordinarily dynamic personal traits and tremendous strength of will. Georgetown County rice barons and their children were often quite obsessive and possessive, and these long-gone personalities account for many of the hauntings in the region.

Whatever the reason for the concentration of spirit activity in the region, almost all of the ghosts of Georgetown have a thrilling story to tell.

Ghosts

of

Georgetown

North Island
Lighthouse

——— · · · ———

ACROSS WINYAH BAY from picturesque and proper Georgetown harbor lies wild, beautiful North Island.

The island is bordered on the south by the shipping channel that connects Georgetown harbor and Winyah Bay to the ocean. On the west, there are miles of salt marshes; on the north, North Inlet, and on the east, the Atlantic Ocean. North Island is accessible only by boat.

Although comprised of no more than sixteen square miles, North Island is a cornucopia of geographical delights.

The salt marshes that form the island's western half are mazed by a labyrinth of channels that lead to her center.

There the high ground is densely wooded with rustling palmetto trees, fragrant cedars, towering pines, and gnarled, ancient, moss-draped oaks.

Her eastern half is lined with deserted, sandy beaches, broken only by the jetty of huge, grey rocks which jut into the Atlantic, forming the north side of the shipping channel.

Across the shipping channel from North Island lies South Island. A jetty that extends from South Island lines the south side of the shipping channel.

Breathtaking by day and enchanting by night, North Island is as changeable as she is lovely. A peaceful, calm morning can become a howling afternoon, changing the idyllic island into a storm-ravaged atoll nearly devoid of shelter.

Many recreational boaters who have ignored weather forecasts have traveled across the bay to North Island with ease, only to have a rough and treacherous return crossing—if they were able to return at all.

Long ago, before there were satellites, weather radar, and storm warnings, the captains of great wooden fishing boats piloted their crafts out of Georgetown harbor, crossed Winyah Bay, and headed out into the Atlantic. Only their instincts and their knowledge of the changing weather patterns alerted them to forthcoming storms.

NOAA, so heavily relied upon by modern mariners, was yet to be established. Great storms could rush into the south Atlantic with virtually no warning.

A quiet, clear day, bringing hauls of shrimp which filled

the nets, would give no indication that a fierce storm would soon blow in from the ocean.

Such a calm, prosperous day was the setting decades ago when a young boy, now an experienced captain with a large commercial boat of his own, was hard at work on a shrimp trawler in the Atlantic off North Island.

The lad had recently moved with his family to Georgetown from the Midwest. He found his new job on the big shrimp boat hard, but enjoyable.

The captain, although strict, was a fair, good man who made sure that every crew member on his boat was treated equally.

The boy looked forward to each trip out of the harbor, anticipating the moment when they would clear the jetties and be out in the rolling Atlantic.

On some trips, the captain took the trawler and her crew far up or down the coast, depending on the time of year and where the shrimp were running. On other trips, such as this one, they let their nets down closer to home.

Either way, the boy always enjoyed the time spent at sea.

On this particular afternoon, the great wooden boat was trawling in the ocean just out of sight of North Island, having put out of Georgetown harbor that morning before dawn. The sun was high in the bright blue sky, the sea was calm, and the shrimping was good.

The lad was hard at work on the wide aft deck of the boat, separating thousands of shrimp from yet another large haul drawn in by the crew.

He rarely looked up, knowing that the ocean, except for

the silhouettes of other fishing boats, was the only thing on the horizon for as far as he could see in any direction.

Momentarily alone at his work, concentrating hard on doing it quickly, the boy suddenly jerked his head up as a movement caught his eye.

Standing near the boat's transom was a young girl. Her long, blond hair was caught up with a pink ribbon. The ruffled hem of her pink ankle-length dress moved gently with the faint ocean breeze. In her hand, the girl held a cloth doll.

The boy was too surprised to speak. Where had she come from? He wanted to tell the pretty child that she shouldn't be standing on the transom — she could fall off — but he could not make a sound.

Staring hard at him, the girl said, "Go back." She raised the arm that was not holding the doll and pointed toward the jetties. "Go back."

Dropping shrimp from both gloved hands, the boy jumped up and looked around wildly. Where were his fellow crew members when he needed them? When he looked back toward the stern, she was gone.

He ran over to the stern and looked down into the blue-grey water, even though he had heard no splash.

There was no sign of her.

Greatly disturbed, he ran to tell the captain.

The boy found the captain in the wheelhouse, preparing to turn the trawler east toward the sea.

"What is it, young fellow?" the bearded older man asked, concern knitting his brow as he looked at the trembling youngster.

The boy blurted out his story, then looked down. Perhaps, he thought, he should have kept quiet. Even to his own ears, his experience sounded daft. The captain will think I have taken leave of my senses, he thought. Consumed by regret and confusion, he looked up to find the captain staring sternly at him.

"Thank you, son," he said quietly. "We'll be heading in now."

The boy asked for no explanation, nor was he given one.

"We're heading in," was all the captain told his surprised crew.

Although a few of the men raised their eyebrows and exchanged questioning glances, they all began preparing to put in immediately.

Soon the big white shrimp trawler was headed west, toward the Georgetown jetties and home.

To every boat that passed within hailing distance, the captain, his voice deep and booming, shouted, "Bad storm coming! Head on in!"

The captain's warning went unheeded. None of the other boat captains were willing to abandon such good shrimping on a calm day because of rumored bad weather.

Later that afternoon, as the boat passed through the wide channel between the jetties, dark clouds gathered rapidly and a stiff breeze blew.

The rising tide nearly concealed the great, granite jetty rocks. Only the jagged stone points were visible above the swirling water.

To starboard, lovely North Island darkened in unison with the rapidly blackening sky.

Set back from the golden sand of the island's south beach, the base of the lighthouse was ghostly pale against the dark trees. Into the charcoal-grey firmament rose the luminous pearly tower, its beacon shining brightly.

The boy leaned hard against the starboard bow rail and gazed intently at the lighthouse. It was one of his favorite sights, but he was not in the mood to enjoy it. Seeing the little girl had been unsettling to him. Baffled and deep in thought, he did not hear the captain walk up behind him.

The older gentleman placed his hand on the boy's shoulder and smiled apologetically as the lad gave a start. He nodded his grey head toward the lighthouse. "That was her home."

Thus began the captain's story.

. . .

In the 1790's, the United States government began to construct a series of lighthouses as navigational aides for the increasing sea trade.

At this time, the only two lighthouses along the south Atlantic coast were at Tybee Island, Georgia, and Morris Island, near the entrance to Charleston harbor.

The people of Georgetown were eager to have a lighthouse to mark the entrance to their harbor. Approaching and crossing Winyah Bay was difficult because of the many dangerous shoals. Without a beacon to guide them in, ships did well not to run aground.

A lighthouse would not only mark the entrance to Winyah

Bay, it would also serve as a landmark for ship pilots making the hazardous crossing.

In 1795, Congress approved the money for a lighthouse on North Island. After delays over land acquisition, construction on the lighthouse finally began in 1798.

The amount of money given for construction of the lighthouse dictated that it would be built of wood, as were most other lighthouses of this time. The superintendent of the Charleston lighthouse was placed in charge of constructing the Georgetown structure.

Plans were made for a seventy-two-foot-high wooden tower with an eight-sided, brick base. Close to the peak of the tower, a six-foot-wide iron lantern, enclosed in a clear heavy glass, would rest on a wide platform. A trap door would lead from the lantern room into the body of the tower, where five flights of stairs would descend to the ground.

By the end of 1800, the carpenter had finished his work, and statewide newspapers reported that the finished lighthouse glowed with "a full and brilliant light."

In 1806, a terrible storm destroyed the wooden lighthouse. Shortly thereafter, Congress appropriated money for a new lighthouse, specifying that it must be constructed of brick or stone.

The new lighthouse was operational by 1812. Except for thick stone in place of wood, few alterations were made from the plans of the original lighthouse.

Over the next century, the North Island lighthouse, also known as the Georgetown Light, had a succession of keepers. Most stayed for years. Cozy living quarters were provided at the lighthouse. The keeper could fulfill his important duty of tending the light and maintaining the lighthouse, while enjoying magnificent isolation of North Island with his family.

One lighthouse keeper lived there with his small daughter. The child—a cheerful, pretty blond—was a delight to her father, who loved her dearly.

About twice a month, the father and daughter took their rowboat to Georgetown for supplies. They had to make sure to go with the tide. Rowing against the current in Winyah Bay was arduous, difficult, and usually unnecessary if they timed their departures correctly. These visits would only last a few hours because the lighthouse keeper had to return to the island in time to light the great whale-oil lantern before dark.

One fateful day, just before dawn, the lighthouse keeper and his daughter set out for Georgetown.

The little girl sat happily in the bow of the rowboat, holding her favorite rag doll. She joked merrily with her father as he rowed. She always looked forward to these trips because she could spend time with her father in town.

The pair crossed the bay and approached the Georgetown waterfront. The sun climbed into the bright blue sky, as it rose over the ocean on their port side.

Upon reaching the harbor and tying up their rowboat, the lighthouse keeper and the child disembarked and walked down the dock into town.

When it was time to return to the lighthouse that afternoon, the lighthouse keeper felt a bit uneasy about the wind that had come up while they were in town. It was not a fierce wind, and worrying about it was fruitless because they had to get back to the lighthouse in time to light the lantern.

The keeper helped his daughter into the rowboat. The little girl laid her doll in the bow of the boat and helped her father load the supplies. As he pushed off from the dock and rowed out of sight of Georgetown, he hoped the dark rain clouds that gathered above him would not burst before he and his daughter reached North Island.

By the time they were more than three-quarters of the way home, the lighthouse keeper was overcome with exhaustion. Although he was rowing with the outgoing tide, the wind that blew against him grew stronger and stronger.

The wind grew fiercer, as did the water in the bay. Waves began to crash into the little boat, quickly swamping it.

As the rain and hail pelted their bodies, the lighthouse keeper untied the bowline from the rapidly sinking rowboat and used it to tie himself to his little daughter.

When the boat sank, he swam with his little girl tied to his back. His only hope was to reach South Island. If only he had known a horrible storm was coming, he thought. If only he had kept his little daughter safe in Georgetown.

Nearly overcome by exhaustion and shock, the lighthouse keeper did not remember the sky growing dark. Neither did he remember crawling up and collapsing on the north shore of South Island, his beloved child still tied firmly to his back.

When he awoke early the next morning, his little

daughter was dead. She had drowned while her father desperately tried to save their lives.

The poor man was inconsolable. He was never the same after losing his little girl. For a long time afterward, he wandered the streets of Georgetown, sad and disoriented, calling out the name of his dead child.

. . .

The captain had heard this story when he was a young man, and he knew that the ghost of the little girl often warned sailors when a violent storm was preparing to sweep into the bay. That is why, he explained, he took the boy's incredible story so seriously.

After the shrimp trawler's safe arrival in Georgetown that day, the storm worsened steadily. By dark, the storm had reached a terrible crescendo. Many boats and lives were lost in the deadly storm.

The boy never forgot his chilling experience, or a word of the captain's story.

Now a well-seasoned, grey-bearded captain with his own successful commercial boat, he can sometimes be persuaded to tell of the afternoon he met the ghost of the little girl from the North Island lighthouse.

North Island is located on the Atlantic Ocean at the entrance of Winyah Bay.

The
Sunset Lodge

——— . . . ———

ONE QUIET AFTERNOON, Bettye Marsh and her sister-in-law sat in the parlor of Bettye's home. They were trying to imagine all the clandestine meetings and breathless liaisons that must have taken place in the room where they now sat.

Bettye's home had a livelier history than the homes of most people. Her family's comfortable, white clapboard house was once known as the Sunset Lodge, one of the country's most famous bordellos.

Bettye and her sister-in-law laughingly discussed the huge, beveled plate-glass mirror that hung in the parlor. Every morning, before she took the curlers out of her hair, Bettye passed by the mirror on her way to the kitchen. She knew that Miss Hazel, the legendary madam who founded Sunset Lodge, originally hung the mirror in the parlor. Miss Hazel was strict about the appearance of the girls in her bordello, and she would not allow them to enter the parlor before completing an immaculate toilette from head to toe. Only the image of elaborately coiffed, elegantly dressed ladies of the evening had been reflected in the mirror during the years the house was a bordello.

"Isn't it funny," Bettye said to her sister-in-law with a giggle, "that the mirror now reflects me every morning in my robe and curlers!"

The old house was perfectly still and absolutely quiet as the two women discussed the scandalous history of Sunset Lodge. Not so much as a breeze stirred outside.

Suddenly the huge mirror crashed to the floor! The wind had not blown. The ground had not trembled, nor had any door slammed. The mirror, which had hung securely for years, simply fell.

Bettye and her sister-in-law sprang from their seats and rushed over to examine the fallen mirror.

The strong, heavy wire which supported the mirror was unbroken. The screws holding the wire in place were still fixed to the back of the mirror. The nail upon which the mirror hung was firmly imbedded in the wall.

There was no explanation for the falling mirror. Finally, the girls realized that they should not have been joking about the past of Sunset Lodge. The ghost of Miss Hazel was known to still wander the halls of the old bordello.

Obviously, the women's light-hearted discussion offended her, and her spirit knocked the mirror off the wall to remind them that they should discuss her home's history with greater reverence.

. . .

The story of Sunset Lodge began one fine day, years before the Second World War. Hazel Weisse of French Lick, Indiana, was hard at work in her annual spring-cleaning.

She had just finished painstakingly washing all of her quilts and hanging them on the clothesline to dry when the clothesline broke. All of Hazel's wet wash was pitched into the dirt.

This was a definitive moment in Hazel's life. She took the snapping of the clothesline as a sign that it was time to change her difficult lifestyle.

Hazel was a widow who was raising her son single-handedly. She was also the parent for the three orphaned children of her dead sister. Hazel could barely keep these four children clothed and fed. As if this was not enough of a job for one woman, Hazel was also a full-time school-teacher.

That spring afternoon, when all of her clean quilts fell into the dirt, Hazel decided she was going to have to find another way to support her family.

Before too long, Hazel had a new career as a madam in a genteel bordello in Florence, South Carolina.

Around 1936, the great Georgetown paper mill was being built. Everyone in town knew this mill would provide a great boost for Georgetown's economy. Many workers came to Georgetown from large northern cities to help construct the huge mill. The construction of the mill would take the workers a long time. Town fathers in Georgetown decided that a bordello would be a good way to keep this large work force off the streets and out of trouble.

According to local tradition, Tom Yawkey, a wealthy Northern businessman, was enlisted to help create the Georgetown bordello.

Yawkey, who was the owner of the Boston Red Sox, also owned South Island and spent part of the winter at his home there. He usually came south to Florence by train, then proceeded to Georgetown by car.

During one of his trips to Florence, he made the acquaintance of Hazel Weisse. Since Georgetown was in need of a brothel and someone to run it, he persuaded Hazel to set up her business there.

Now that a madame for the bordello was found, the town fathers set out to find the perfect location. They finally settled on property just outside of the town limits. The only problem with the location was that the property was owned by a woman named Annie Sisson. Sisson had purchased the land two years earlier for $250. Since then, she had built a two-story house on the land and did not have the property on the market.

In order to convince her to sell, the tradition continues, town fathers told Sisson that her mortgage would be foreclosed if she did not cooperate. Annie Sisson was reputed to be one of the principal bootleggers in Georgetown County, and since prohibition was still in effect, she was vulnerable to town leaders' wishes.

In 1936, Miss Hazel, as Hazel Weisse came to be known, bought the property from Annie Sisson and set out to make the Sunset Lodge a grand success.

All of the women Miss Hazel hired were attractive, well-mannered, and refined. None of them were local. In order to hide their profession from their families, all of the Sunset Lodge ladies told their relatives they worked at a resort lodge. They made sure that they visited their families instead of vice-versa.

Miss Hazel did not receive her relatives at the Sunset Lodge either. She kept an apartment in Charleston, about sixty miles south of Georgetown, where she visited with her family.

The girls employed by Miss Hazel, numbering sometimes as many as eighteen, were always examples of good health. At Miss Hazel's insistence, all of the girls had a blood test once a month and went to the doctor once a week. Each girl had a certificate of health displayed under glass on top of her dresser or bedside table.

Miss Hazel's girls did not go into town except to visit the doctor. One girl was a beautician and styled the hair of the other girls. Anything they needed to buy from town was ordered by telephone. The girls made a good living at Sunset Lodge, and they helped support the Georgetown economy with many purchases from local merchants. Miss Hazel purchased a new car each year from a local dealership. Many of the other girls also bought automobiles in Georgetown. The girls often ordered dresses and lingerie from local dress shops. They also ordered many toys. In fact, one resident opened a toy shop mainly to fill the requests of the Sunset Lodge ladies. (When the lodge finally closed, his business fell so sharply that he had to close the shop.)

During World War II, many servicemen visited the lodge when they were in the area. The servicemen then scattered throughout the world to fight the war, and the fame of the Sunset Lodge grew far and wide.

After World War II, Miss Hazel's bordello established a reputation as a frolicsome diversion for the affluent. Doctors, lawyers, state and local officials, and many other professionals made up most of her clientele.

Greater international fame came to the Sunset Lodge from its proximity to Georgetown's seaport. The captains and navigators of merchant ships were w 'come at the bordello, but the crews were not.

When Tom Yawkey stopped over on South Island with the Boston Red Sox, on their way to Florida for spring training, he brought Miss Hazel's girls to the island. Many of Yawkey's wealthy friends visited him on the island in their yachts. Occasionally they would pick up one of the girls there and embark on cruises around the world. When the cruises were over, the wealthy patrons would pay for the girls to fly back to South Carolina. The girls would take a taxi from the airport in Columbia back to Georgetown.

Bettye Marsh's late husband, Jack, owned the taxi service that brought the girls back from Columbia. A former Georgetown police officer, Jack had known Miss Hazel for years. When he opened his taxi company, a great deal of his business consisted of ferrying guests to and from Sunset Lodge. Many of these guests were locals who preferred to visit the bordello by taxi rather than run the risk of having their cars seen there.

The heyday of Sunset Lodge came to an abrupt end several days before Christmas in 1969, when Sheriff Woodrow Carter decreed that it must close. This order was so sudden that the girls had only a matter of hours to collect their belongings and leave.

No one knows what precipitated this blunt ending of an era, but one thing was definite — the Sunset Lodge was no longer in business.

None of the women had time to find boxes and pack. Most of them carried their personal property away in dresser drawers.

By this time, Miss Hazel was an invalid. Bedridden and failing in health, she feared that she would not be able to answer the door to give customers the sad news that the lodge was closed.

While she was trying to decide what to do, Miss Hazel asked Jack Marsh to stay at the lodge. Then she asked Bettye and the children to move in, too. After they were settled, Miss Hazel said that she would sell them the property if she could stay in her upstairs apartment.

Bettye and Jack bought the property in 1970. Miss Hazel and a servant lived in the upstairs apartment for two more years.

Nearly all of the girls came back to visit Miss Hazel and return the dresser drawers. Sometimes they would call first to ask Bettye's permission before coming to visit.

Bettye and Miss Hazel became good friends. Bettye's son and daughter were like grandchildren to the former madam.

By the early 1990's, the lodge had been closed for over two decades, but polite, well-mannered men, usually driving expensive cars, still stopped by looking for the famous bordello.

Miss Hazel died several years after the lodge closed but her ghost continued to reside in the house. The Marshes would often hear doors opening and closing upstairs in Miss Hazel's former quarters when they knew there was no one else in the house. The Marshes believed Miss Hazel continued to watch over her home. Bettye didn't wish to offend the kind old woman, and, after the mirror fell in the parlor, she never again made fun of the Sunset Lodge's colorful history.

. . .

A few months after the 24th anniversary of the lodge's abrupt closing, a fire burned the former Sunset Lodge to the ground. While the adjacent apartments, including the former quarters of the famous lodge girls, were left standing, the main house was destroyed.

Bettye Marshe lost her home of nearly a quarter century, and Georgetown lost a legendary monument.

The remains of the Sunset Lodge are on the west side of U.S.17, a few hundred feet south of Georgetown's city limits.

Daisy Bank

— · · · —

WHILE MANY OF Georgetown's rice plantations have stood since the eighteenth century, enduring events as devastating as the Civil War and major hurricanes, others have slid into oblivion.

As land changed hands and new owners merged their holdings during the decades after the Civil War, some of the plantations were lost in the process.

One of these long-gone jewels was named Daisy Bank. Although the house and gardens of this once-thriving plantation have disappeared, the legend of the ghost of Daisy Bank remains.

During the early part of the nineteenth century, Daisy Bank Plantation was the home of a former sea captain who had given up life on the high seas for the love of a Georgetown belle. In order to win her hand, he traded the responsibilities of a ship and crew for those of a rice plantation.

As a plantation owner, the former captain could stay close by his bride and provide her with the lifestyle she deserved.

The couple's blissful life together was soon highlighted by the discovery that the young mistress of Daisy Bank was expecting a baby. The couple joyously anticipated the birth of their first child.

However, their happiness was shattered when the mistress of Daisy Bank died in childbirth. Her husband was distraught. Although he knew it was inevitable, the bereaved captain could not bear the thought of burying his lovely wife.

Grievously, he began to plan her internment.

A six-foot grave was dug beneath the branches of a live oak tree. According to the plantation owner's specifications, the bottom and sides were lined with brick.

Obsessed with the need to preserve his wife's exquisite beauty, the captain ordered a form-fitting casket for her body. After she was lovingly placed in the custom coffin, a glass cover was laid on top. All of the air was drawn out of the casket before the glass lid was permanently sealed shut.

Once his beloved was ensconced in her sarcophagus, the distraught widower refused to allow anyone to move his wife's body from their once-happy house. Finally, at the insistence of family and close friends, his wife was placed at the bottom of her brick vault.

A slab of marble was laid across the top of the tomb,

giving the grave the outward appearance of a typical low country burial site. But this one was unique. If the marble slab was removed, the mistress of Daisy Bank was visible in her final resting place.

The widower threw himself into running the plantation. He had acquired Daisy Bank because of his bride. Now he would continue to care for it in memory of her.

Every evening after supper, he walked down to the grave under the live oak and removed the marble slab. Then he sat on the edge of the vault, close to where his wife lay. This ritual became an important part of the planter's daily routine. Sitting by the vault where he could view his wife's preserved form was the way he ended each day for the rest of his life.

After the planter's death, Daisy Bank was incorporated into neighboring Annandale Plantation.

It was not long before black folks from Annandale began avoiding the Daisy Bank gravesite after dark.

The old master of Daisy Bank, they said, still visited his wife's grave in the evenings.

Danky, a black gentleman born in 1872, was one of the few black people who would walk through Daisy Bank at night. Any evening that Danky passed close to the grave-site, he never failed to see the old master of Daisy Bank sitting by the tomb of his wife.

Danky would always tip his hat and say to the spirit, "Good evening, sir," and keep on walking.

Other people from Annandale, however, would walk quite a bit out of their way to avoid passing anywhere near the Daisy Bank gravesite after dark. These individuals dreaded seeing the old master's spirit because they feared it. It was whispered that he would rise from his seat beside his wife's grave and chase anyone who broke into a panicky run.

When the spirit got close enough in the chase, it was said that he would jump on the back of the terrified runner.

As the years passed, the Daisy Bank plantation house fell into disrepair and was torn down. Even its foundation of handmade brick was dismantled and taken to the upper part of the state.

During hard times, many Georgetown rice plantations were sold to wealthy Northerners who restored the plantation homes and used their vast grounds for hunting.

According to local tradition, a young man and woman who had strayed from a visiting hunting party stumbled upon the overgrown gravesite at Daisy Bank.

The couple sat down to drink from the young man's whiskey flask, using the raised marble slab that covered the mistress' vault as a convenient resting place. When they found that the marble cover would move, the curious pair pushed it aside and discovered the forgotten glassed-in coffin. Like an enchanted doll, the plantation owner's wife still rested in her sealed enclosure.

Seeing a bracelet on the arm of the corpse, the couple decided to break the glass and steal the jewels. Under the influence of whiskey and youthful foolishness, they reached down and thrust their rifle butts through the glass cover. But when the heavy glass shattered, the lady's entire body instantly dissolved into dust.

As if a spell had broken, the young intruders immediately regretted their action.

Disturbed and ashamed, they left the old gravesite. Although no one knows whether there was any connection between the grave-robbing incident or not, it is known that both intruders met mysterious deaths not long after their hunting trip to Daisy Bank.

Several years ago a young man arrived at the Annandale plantation seeking permission to move the old grave. The emissary explained that he represented the neice of the mistress of Daisy Bank. His client wished to move her relative to a less deserted location.

Permission was granted, and the grave was moved. It now lies near Charleston, in Mount Pleasant's lovely Christ Church Cemetery.

Since the spirit of the master of Daisy Bank has not been seen for a long time now, perhaps seeing his wife at rest in such a peaceful place has allowed his soul to also rest.

*The former site of Daisy Bank is located
off South Island Road, several miles south of Georgetown.
It is not visible from the road.*

Pelican Inn of Pawleys Island

———— . . . ————

PERHAPS THE MOST frequently told ghost story in Georgetown County is that of the Grey Man.

According to numerous documented accounts, he appears on the beach at Pawleys Island prior to hurricanes. Everyone who has seen the Grey Man says that he warns them to leave the island.

Residents who are wise enough to heed the Grey Man's warning always find their homes undamaged after the storm. Encounters with the Grey Man have taken place before every major hurricane that has struck the island for more than a hundred years.

The Grey Man is unquestionably a permanent resident of Pawleys Island, but what causes this kind spirit to warn unsuspecting residents of approaching danger? The answer may lie in one of three different accounts that exist about the origin of the Grey Man.

According to one legend, a young woman was walking the windswept, lonely beach not far from her parents' Pawleys Island home.

She was in mourning for her childhood sweetheart who had recently died in a tragic accident on the island.

Her love had returned to Georgetown by ship after an absence of several months. He was so eager to see his beloved fiancée that, rather than wasting one more precious moment away from her, he took a shortcut across previously untraveled marshland.

With his faithful manservant riding a short distance behind, the eager fellow and his horse came to a sudden stop and began to sink rapidly into a patch of deadly quicksand. His manservant watched in horror, unable to help his young master, as the young man and his horse disappeared into the mire.

When the young woman heard of her fiancé's tragic death, she was heartbroken.

After the funeral, she took to walking the stretch of beach where she and her beau used to stroll in happier times. This particular day was windier than most, but it suited her recent mood. She was alone with her sadness in the whipping wind, with the ocean crashing by her side.

Suddenly, a figure appeared ahead. As she walked closer,

the young woman could have sworn it was her fiancé. With no fear, she walked toward him.

"Leave the island at once," he said. "You are in danger. Leave the island!"

Then he disappeared.

The young lady hurried home to tell her father and mother about the strange, unsettling experience. Upon hearing their daughter's strange story, her parents immediately began making plans to leave Pawleys Island for their inland home. They did not know what danger they were fleeing, but they did know that their daughter was a sensible person and not prone to flights of fancy.

The family left Pawleys Island before dawn the following morning.

That night, as they lay sleeping in the safety of their inland home, a fierce hurricane ravaged Pawleys Island. The hurricane destroyed most of the homes on Pawleys Island, but the home of the young woman's family was undamaged.

. . .

Another legend about the Grey Man claims that he is the spirit of Plowden Charles Jeannerette Weston, the original owner of the house on Pawleys Island now known as the Pelican Inn.

Born in 1819, Plowden was a member of a wealthy Georgetown rice plantation dynasty. He spent his early years at Laurel Hill Plantation, where he was privately educated by a British tutor.

At the age of twelve, Plowden's family temporarily moved to England so that their son could attend school there. Although the boy's father was adamantly anti-British, he wanted Plowden to have a proper, classical English education.

Eventually, the Weston family returned to the Georgetown area, but Plowden stayed on to study at Cambridge. There, he fell deeply in love with Emily Frances Esdaile, the beautiful sister of one of his close friends.

Emily's father was a English baronet. Plowden feared that his father would not approve of his plans to marry Emily because of his anti-British sentiments and his disdain for British aristocracy. Plowden sailed back to Georgetown to discuss his marriage plans face to face with his father.

Plowden's father agreed to the wedding but trouble soon appeared on the horizon. Emily's father and Plowden's father began to compete to see who could give the young couple the finest wedding present. Emily's father opened the battle by giving them a dowry of seven thousand pounds. Plowden's father arrogantly replied that he would give the couple seventy thousand pounds, a house in London, and one in Geneva. Emily's father quickly realized that he could not compete with the astonishingly rich rice planter.

Despite the animosity between their fathers, Plowden and

Emily were married in August of 1847. They established their residence at Hagley Plantation, another gift from Plowden's father. Hagley was by far the finest gift of all. Its lands included vast acres of fertile rice fields which extended from the black, cypress-lined Waccamaw River to the Atlantic Ocean.

Just off the shore of Hagley Plantation was Pawleys Island, the golden gem of the Waccamaw Neck. Soon after the wedding, Plowden and Emily made plans to build a summer home there.

For years, low country planters made their summer homes on the sea islands to escape the malaria-carrying mosquitoes that plagued the plantations. Plowden and Emily were acclimated to England's cooler weather and were especially anxious to escape the subtropical humidity and intense heat of the plantation summers. They also sought a home where they could take refuge from the social and work-related demands of Hagley Plantation.

The house they built is now known as Pelican Inn.

Renty Tucker, Hagley's master carpenter, was in charge of construction for the Pelican Inn. Every piece of lumber for the island home was hand-hewn and numbered at Hagley before it was taken by boat to Pawleys.

One of the few homes on Pawleys at that time, Pelican Inn was lovingly planned.

Its elevated, strong-timbered foundation and the lower floor were nestled behind the dunes in a tangle of sea oats, cedars, and myrtles. The upper portion of the house rose high above the trees and sheltering dunes. Handmade arches and columns adorned the wide porch that surrounded the lower floor.

The second-floor piazza faced the Atlantic. This porch was accessible from the bedrooms on the upper floor. Plowden and Emily spent many peaceful hours on this high and secluded piazza, gazing at the night sky and the Atlantic Ocean.

Splitting their time between Hagley and their beloved island retreat, the young Westons led a happy, productive, and sometimes secluded, existence.

Plowden and Emily were devout Episcopalians, and they shared a deep concern for the spiritual lives of Hagley's 350 slaves. Unable by law to educate these people, the Westons focused on their spiritual enlightenment.

Plowden and Emily had an exquisite chapel built on Hagley Plantation. The chapel could seat up to two hundred slaves at a time. One of thirteen slave chapels on the Waccamaw Neck, Saint Mary's of Hagley was by far the most lovely. The chapel was adorned with stained-glass windows handcrafted in England, hand-carved oak choir stalls, and a granite baptismal font.

Plowden and Emily spent the first decade of their married lives absorbed in each other, the intricate workings of their plantation, and their scholarly pursuits.

By the late 1850s, however, Plowden began to feel that their productive paradise would not last forever.

In the years before the war, Plowden, a published South Carolina historian, turned his literary and oratory skills toward the dissension that was growing between the North and South. He gave many fiery and prophetic speeches warning of the impending confrontation. Yet, his support always lay with the Southern cause.

When the Civil War began, Plowden turned his attention away from oration and towards battle. He became company commander of the Georgetown Rifle Guard, Company A of the Tenth Regiment. He personally armed, uniformed, and supplied gear to the 150 men that were in his charge.

During the early part of the war, when the future of the Confederacy was more than a hopeful dream, he and Emily entertained many of the regiment's men and their ladies at the Pelican Inn.

Later in the war, an alarm arose for the Rifle Guard to gather within a few miles of Hagley Plantation. When the threat turned into a false alarm, Plowden came up with a wonderful idea.

He sent word to Hagley that his entire company would be arriving that night for dinner. Soon the weary group was enjoying a luxurious three-course dinner, served with family silver, crystal, and fine china for all. Each course arrived with a different vintage of wine from the Hagley cellar.

Near the end of the war, Plowden contracted tuberculosis. Eventually, it worsened to the point that his life was in danger. Fearing that they would lose him, Plowden's friends in the state legislature intervened. They knew Plowden would not leave his command, so these concerned lawmakers elected their old friend to the office of lieutenant governor.

Plowden gave up his command to accept this office, but

he was unable to serve for long. By the end of January 1864, the tuberculosis he contracted during his service to the Confederate army worsened, and it became evident that he would die.

At Plowden's request, each of the Hagley servants traveled to Conway, South Carolina, where he lay dying. There they received from him, one at a time, a small personal gift of remembrance.

His last moments were spent with the love of his life, his adoring Emily. He asked her to arrange for two of their devoted servants to transport his body by canoe down the Waccamaw River to Hagley. He also asked her to see that he was buried next to his father in the churchyard of All Saints' Waccamaw Episcopal Church, the place where he and Emily were married.

It is because of Plowden's faithful service to his beloved home, and those who lived on it, that many believe that he is the Grey Man. The same Plowden Charles Jeannerette Weston who warned his neighbors of the risks of war and later fought for his cherished homeland, now roams the beach near his beloved island home warning residents of impending danger.

• • •

Still another version of the legend of the Grey Man exists.

Mrs. Eileen Weaver, who owned Pelican Inn for many years, has seen the Grey Man many times, but she believes he is someone else—someone she identified from a nineteenth century photograph.

The first time Mrs. Weaver saw a spirit at Pelican Inn,

she was in the kitchen with her cook, preparing homemade bread.

The two women were absorbed in kneading the heavy dough when Mrs. Weaver turned to see a lady standing behind her, arms akimbo and eyes fixed sternly on the breadmaking process.

Her features, Mrs. Weaver said, were French and she wore a disapproving expression. She seemed to be scrutinizing the making of the bread as if to say, "You better do it right."

The woman's dress was made of a material like gingham, patterned in a little grey-and-white check. Her bodice was fronted with tiny pearl buttons, and a long apron was tied at her waist.

Despite the woman's clarity of appearance, Mrs. Weaver could tell the figure standing before her was not a living human.

"You knew the features were not earthly, but they were clear," Weaver explained.

This was only the first of many appearances by the spirit of the woman. She became a somewhat familiar and anticipated sight at Pelican Inn. Mrs. Weaver recalls that some of her guests would wait on the sofa in the spacious sitting room on balmy summer evenings and watch for the woman to walk up the stairs.

Many guests did not realize she was a spirit the first time they saw her.

Mrs. Weaver's first encounter with the spirit she believes to be the Grey Man was as abrupt as her first encounter with the woman. One day, he suddenly appeared in front of her, wearing clothes from the nineteenth century. The male figure also began to appear regularly, and Mrs. Weaver and her family grew used to the two spirits that shared their home.

Mrs. Weaver's daughter relates this occurrence:

> During spring cleaning one year, my sister-in-law, Gayle, was helping my mother get the inn in shape for the summer guests. Her job involved cleaning the upstairs bedroom and hallway. Mother always had magazines and books on a long reading table in the hallway for the enjoyment of the guests. Usually, at the end of the season, all of the magazines would be discarded, but some comic books remained this time from the previous year. Gayle reached to thumb through one. Finding it interesting, she leaned back against the table. This apparently did not set well with the ghosts of the house because after a few moments, Gayle felt a tug at her shirt tail.
>
> Thinking it was one of us teasing her, she ignored the tug and continued to read. Again there was a tug at her shirt tail, and this time she turned around to see who was there. She realized that the wood floors made it impossible for anyone to sneak up on her without being heard. Whoever it was got the message across, because Gayle quickly laid the comic book down and went back to work. It took Gayle some time to tell us this story, but we never doubted that it happened. This type of thing happened on a regular basis around the house.

Mrs. Weaver told her experiences at Pelican Inn to the late chronicler of Georgetown's history, Julian Stevenson Bolick.

He brought her an assortment of nineteenth-century photographs and asked her to look through them. From the many photographs, Mrs. Weaver identified a picture of a woman and another picture of a man who looked unmistakably like the spirits in her home. The pictures she had chosen were photographs of Mr. and Mrs. Mazyck, cousins of Plowden and Emily Weston.

The Westons did not have any children, and when Emily Weston died, the Mazycks inherited the Pelican Inn. The Mazycks lovingly operated the home as a bed-and-breakfast inn for many years. Mrs. Weaver believes the spirit of Mr. Mazyck is the Grey Man.

Whoever the Grey Man is, he continues to patrol the beach of windswept Pawleys Island, appearing prior to deadly hurricanes to warn those who live on the island of impending danger.

The Pawleys Island North Causeway is located 10 miles north of Georgetown on U.S. 17. The Pelican Inn, now a bed-and-breakfast lodge, faces the Atlantic just off the island end of the causeway.

Hagley Landing

———— · · · ————

THE TIME AFTER the War Between the States was a period of grim despondency for once-prosperous Georgetown County.

Many plantation homes and crops were ravaged by Union soldiers in the final days of the war. During the confusion and lawless days of Reconstruction, desolate days continued.

While reunions with loved ones home from the battlefields made material losses seem unimportant to many families, those families left with a permanently empty chair by the fireside faced a bleak future.

Mail service was unreliable during this time, causing long periods of painful worry for families of the Confederate militia. Those at home often did not hear of a loved one's battlefield death or injury until months after the fact. Many a woman did not know that her husband, father, brother, son or fiancé was dead until the wagon bearing his body rolled slowly up the drive.

Still other women experienced the joy of having a loved one ride home unexpectedly, long after all but the faintest shred of hope for his return was gone.

Hagley Landing, the Waccamaw River dockage for Hagley Plantation, was the scene of one unexpected postwar reunion that ended in tragedy.

In the somber and grim days after the war, those who dwelled on Georgetown County's Waccamaw Neck plantations celebrated few happy occasions other than births and weddings.

Nuptial festivities were particularly bittersweet social occasions during those years. The lavish entertainment associated with the marriages of plantation gentry was remembered with poignant clarity. But it was a lifestyle few could now afford.

Several years after the war ended, St. Mary's, the former slave chapel on Hagley Plantation, was the church one young Waccamaw Neck couple chose for their wedding. The bride was engaged before the war. She and her fiancé planned a huge wedding in one of the county's larger Episcopal churches, but the nuptials were postponed when the prospective groom joined the ranks of the Confederate militia.

Confident that the war would not last long, the couple had decided against a small, private ceremony, opting for an elaborately planned ceremony and exuberant festivities after the Confederate militia rode home triumphant.

This was not to be.

As the war dragged on and the Confederate casualties mounted, the bride-to-be longed for word from her beloved but also feared news of his death. Even after most of the Georgetown militia had returned to their homes, she heard nothing. His letters had long since ceased. Hope and anxiety turned to fear and dread.

The young woman's only consolation was her fiancé's best friend, who was equally worried about his missing companion.

The two spent long hours reminiscing over their happy childhood together. The three of them had shared many adventures over the years.

Although she remained devoted to her beloved, the woman began to lose hope after three years of mystery about his fate. Sadly, she faced the reality that he was surely dead.

By this time, the companionship that she shared with his best friend developed into a firm and deep love. First drawn to each other by shared concerns, the couple finally recognized their mutual affection.

With this recognition, the two decided to marry. They were sure their dead loved one would approve and bless their union from his place in heaven.

Their modest wedding in St. Mary's, the former slave chapel at Hagley Plantation, was a well-attended, yet intimate, ceremony. Everyone in the chapel knew what the bride had gone through. There was not a dry eye in the place as the young couple was pronounced man and wife. They were a glowing example of how people could find love and happiness in the aftermath of the war.

After the ceremony, friends and family of the young couple congratulated them outside the church. Happy laughter and cheerful voices drowned out the sound of approaching hoofbeats.

Suddenly, a horse and rider appeared before the chapel. The horse was wet and spent, its flanks heaving. The rider was wearing a tattered Confederate uniform.

He quickly dismounted and surveyed the joyous scene.

The bride gasped and paled as she recognized her beloved fiancé. She approached the man with tears running down her face.

"I waited three years," she said, her low voice filled with anguish. "We didn't know you were still alive. We would never have . . ."

The man in threadbare grey looked slowly from the bride to his best friend and back again. "It will be as if I never came back," he said.

After uttering these words, he ran down to the pier at

Hagley Landing. Never breaking stride, he dashed down its length and leapt off the end into the swift-flowing Waccamaw River. Within seconds he disappeared.

According to local legend, the bride followed the soldier to his watery grave. Then the groom also threw himself into the river and drowned.

Since that fateful day, the romantic trio who met such untimely deaths have been seen many times on the road leading down to Hagley Landing.

The earliest recorded sighting of the ghostly threesome was in 1918, when a young man slammed on the brakes of his car to narrowly miss three unusually dressed figures. The trio vanished before his eyes.

The people he watched vanish into the night were a bride and groom in old-fashioned dress, accompanying what appeared to be a Confederate soldier.

Since 1918, these three spirits have been seen time and time again. Sometimes the bride and groom are hand-in-hand. At other times, all three are strolling together.

Always, these three tragic spirits from another time are reliving what was undoubtedly the most tortured time of their short, young lives.

Hagley Landing is located on the Waccamaw River off of U.S. 17, approximately 11 miles north of Georgetown.

The Witch of
Pawleys Island

———— · · · ————

MANY GHOSTLY LEGENDS have a tangible part, a definitive object that can be seen and touched. Often there is a standing historic home or gravestone to complement the legendary spirit of a life too dynamic to go quietly into the afterworld.

Of some tales of spirit hauntings, however, there is left on this earth only the legend and the spirit, for the home and other hard facts have been lost to the natural elements or the passage of time.

One such legend is that of the Witch of Pawleys Island.

The south end of Pawleys Island is one of the prettiest unspoiled beaches in the Southeast.

The southernmost finger of land on the island is bordered on the east by the Atlantic, on the west by Pawleys Creek, and on the southern end by the wide swash that connects the ocean to the creek.

The area directly across the creek from Pawleys Island is known as mainland Pawleys.

Long, long ago there lived on Pawleys Island a friendly, happy widow. Her home was one of the largest oceanside dwellings on the island.

The affable widow lived a comfortable, pleasant existence. She had lived on the island her entire life. As a young girl, she would spend her days roaming the island with the family's cook, looking for spices and herbs that could be found naturally in the wilds. The old cook taught her how to use these herbs and spices for cooking and home remedies. As the girl grew up, she was often consulted by other inhabitants of the island on what the cook had taught her. The woman was glad to share what she had been taught, and she was quite social with all her neighbors.

Unfortunately, the woman became consumed with a demonic desire that soon destroyed her life.

This fiendish predilection was a preternatural love for great and frequent quantities of whiskey. The widow's relationship with the devilish liquid caused her to abandon all appearances of a normal life in favor of any fiery brew she could find.

She eventually lost her oceanside home on the island and

took up residence in a decrepit shack on the mainland, just across Pawleys Creek from the south end of the island.

When the widow would leave her shack to gather firewood, wild roots, and berries for her cupboard, or make her occasional excursion to Georgetown, people were shocked and sometimes frightened by her appearance. Her threadbare clothing was dyed black to disguise its aged and worn appearance. The widow's long, grey hair was never trimmed, braided, or brushed. It hung in mats and tangles all around her shoulders. Her face was hidden by an old, black hat that cast a shadow around the top part of her body.

Anyone brave or curious enough to attract the old widow's attention received a great shock. She raised her head and looked them full in the eye, mesmerizing them before she let loose a high and earsplitting laugh. Her raucous cackle would shake the hairs on the huge moles that grew on her bulbous nose.

Stories about the strange, evil-looking widow began to spring up on the island, on the mainland, and even in Georgetown.

The very people who once consulted the woman for home remedies and cures now began to spread rumors about her. She was a witch, people whispered, a conjure woman. She had powers. Living out there in that old tumble-down shack, she could "do things."

As rumors about the "witch" circulated, a shy, lovesick young man from Georgetown, eager to win the affections of a young lady he was apprehensive about courting, got the idea that maybe the old hag could do something to help his situation.

Very early one morning—for he did not want to be caught at the woman's shack in the dark—he saddled his horse and set out for Pawleys. By midday, he managed to find the old woman's shack. With more than a little trepidation, he approached the weathered, wooden door of her cabin and raised his hand to knock.

Just as his knuckles hit the grey boards, the door jerked open. The old widow's face appeared not two feet from his own. The bashful young man backed up as the woman's putrid, stale-whiskey breath hit him in the face. He saw the hairy moles on her nose quiver as she curled her lip into a evil grin and gave forth a shrieking laugh.

Squaring his shoulders and trying to remain calm, the fellow said in a shaking voice, "I need a love potion."

The old woman narrowed her eyes shrewdly. A love potion, eh? During those happy days roaming the dunes, the old maum had not only taught the little girl about cooking and remedies. She had also taught her all about hexing, removing hexes, how spells were done according to the phases of the moon and the tides, about the powers of plants and animals. Although the old woman never used this knowledge, she remembered it all.

"How much?" The young man's quavering voice brought her back to the present.

The widow frowned and thought hard.

The moon was still on the increase and there was less than a week before it would be full.

Yesterday, the tide was just beginning to turn and come in at sundown. In two days it would be well on the rise when the sun set. She considered her herb garden. All the raw materials she needed were close at hand.

The young man took some comfort in her hesitation. He found that his voice came out of his throat with a little less effort as he nervously asked once more, "How much?"

The old widow did not hesitate before answering. She knew what she valued most in the world.

"A bottle of whiskey," she croaked, "two days from now at sundown."

Dismissing the uneasy boy with a careless motion of her hand, she slammed the door so hard that its loosely fastened boards trembled.

The young man was thankful to be excused so abruptly. He stepped away backward, reluctant to take his eyes from the weathered grey door lest it fly open and the old banshee spring out after him.

Half of his ordeal was over. The other half was yet to come, two days hence. Then he would have his love potion, and soon after, his heart's desire. Courting that sweet, lovely girl would be an easy task then.

Two days later, at sundown, the old widow was in front of her shack stirring the contents of a black cauldron that steamed over a fire when the young man arrived.

He approached the widow cautiously and, upon reaching her fire, carefully placed a paper sack containing a bottle on the ground beside her.

She looked at the paper sack and nodded her head in

acknowledgment. Then she glared hard into the young man's eyes before she began to speak.

"The potion is ready," the old widow growled, pointing the long, gnarled stirring stick at the young man.

As he backed up, the widow raised the stick toward the twilight sky and gestured at the rising, almost-full moon. "The moon be on the increase and the tide be on the rise," she cackled, swinging her knobby stick toward the ocean that lay across the marsh.

"Now you must do the rest," said the widow, once more glaring at the young man.

She pulled a bottle of clear, brownish-red liquid from the folds of her threadbare black cloak.

"Drink half of this," she demanded, thrusting the corked bottle at the trembling fellow. "Drink!"

The moon was rising over the cold and black-looking Atlantic, whose waves crashed on the shore a mile away. Grey and silver clouds rushed across the darkening, slate-blue sky at a rapid rate. The wind blew hard around the shack, raising its shingles and causing its door to bang. The wind whipped the old widow's cloaks and her unkempt long, grey hair.

The young man fought back the desire to rush to his horse and leave this haunted place.

"Drink!" she shrieked to the young man as the wind whistled past his ears.

Mesmerized and shaking, he snatched the cork off the bottle and drank deeply, fearing the worst.

To his great surprise, the mysterious liquid tasted good.

It was very much like tea. There was something different about it, though—an exotic flavor that he could not quite place, and a hint of mint.

As he took the bottle from his lips, a warm glow spread all over his insides.

He looked at the old widow curiously.

She pointed the gnarled stick at him once more. "Before the moon is full, see that the girl drinks the rest of it. You had half, she gets half. And see that the tide be on the rise when she drinks it. You do as I say, and she will be yours."

Before the young man could reply, the old widow whirled away and was in her shack with the door shut.

As he walked slowly toward his horse, the young man looked down at the bottle in his hand. Although it seemed as if he had swallowed half of the contents, he had only drunk about a fourth of it. Maybe he would save the rest of his half and drink it tomorrow, he thought, right before he called on the young lady he was already considering his.

The stuff surely did make him feel brave. He knew it would make her fall in love with him.

The next day, the young man, still feeling the courage of the night before, decided not to drink the rest of his share. If he gave the young lady three-fourths of the bottle instead of half, he reasoned, then surely it would make her love for him even stronger. Later that afternoon, he called on his beloved and slipped the potion in her tea while she was not looking.

The potion took effect immediately! The young woman fell madly in love with the suitor and before long they were engaged. At first, the young man was ecstatic, but soon he found that his ardor had cooled. While the young woman was devoted to him, he began to find that he could hardly stand the sight of her. He broke the engagement, but the young woman went mad and followed him everywhere. He soon realized that the only way to be rid of her was to leave town without a trace. When the young lady learned of her beloved's disappearance she drowned herself in the ocean; the young man was never heard from again.

Despite the tragic consequences, news of the old hag's potion became known to many on Pawleys Island. Word of mouth soon had her very busy, concocting potions and working spells for the lovesick as well as the vengeful.

Many nights, the fire outside her shack burned well into the night, and the old woman's silhouette could be seen passing back and forth in front of it.

Often, late at night, by the light of her fire, the old crone appeared to be digging. However, no one dared to approach her shack late in the night to find out what it was she was burying.

When the old widow died, it was generally assumed by the people of the Pawleys Island community that she had a carefully hoarded cache of money or valuables hidden away in her shack.

After all, even though most folks who called on her for personal reasons adamantly denied ever approaching the old witch, it was well known that she was supported by a busy magical practice.

Besides that, everyone knew the old widow came from a very wealthy family and had been quite well-off in her own right long ago. Perhaps she had not lost all her fortune after all.

After the widow's shack was thoroughly searched and left to the elements, the grounds around the place became overgrown with tangled weeds and bushes. Possums and deer roamed freely around the old shack, as did other wild creatures.

However, rumors of the widow's late-night diggings, and speculations on what had happened to her secret cache, persisted. Many believed that her secret treasure still lay hidden near her shack, and furtive individuals continued to trek to the site. Hoping to guard their discovery, seekers never went there except under cover of the blackest night.

Many times, a hopeful digger would thrill to the clink of his shovel meeting a hard, solid object, but each time such an object was unearthed, it turned out to be a jug or bottle of whiskey.

Finally, the digging and the searching around the long-gone widow's tumbled-down cabin stopped. No one ever dug up any money or treasure, and, besides, there were too many unexplained noises around the old shack. The horrible growls and cackling howls coming from the surrounding trees made it impossible to concentrate on digging.

Today, the southernmost point of Pawleys Island is often deserted late at night.

Very little artificial light is used there because of nesting sea turtles, who find man-made lights in the night extremely confusing.

In the darkness by the Atlantic, standing on the sandy rise that slopes down to Pawleys Creek, one can still sometimes see the light of a fire across the creek in the darkened, wooded part of the mainland.

If one watches long enough, a silhouette can be seen occasionally passing in front of the fire.

On a very still night, or when the wind is blowing from the west, one may even hear the high, eerie, blood-chilling, cackling laugh of the old widow woman.

The north causeway leading to Pawleys Island
begins approximately 10 miles
north of Georgetown on U.S. 17.

The Litchfield
Manor House

———— · · · ————

IF A TRAVELER wishes to spend the night in a beautiful, haunted, historical manor house, the stately home built by the earliest owner of Litchfield Plantation is a grand place to do so.

The original mansion, the Litchfield manor house, is one of the oldest plantations on the Waccamaw River. The manor house, as well as the surrounding grounds, retains all the qualities of the most cinematic antebellum ideal.

To reach the manor house, a traveler must first pass through the lovely old brick-and-wrought-iron gate entrance, then state intentions to the gatekeeper when he emerges from the weathered brick gatehouse.

The impression the traveler receives when driving toward the house through the quarter-mile tunnel of massive, ancient, moss-draped oak trees is one of isolated splendor.

Emerging from the deep green light of the oak-lined drive into the sunshine that bathes the wide front lawn, the traveler will find that the avenue divides to form a circular drive. This circle closes at the base of wide brick steps that lead up to the white-columned, two-story veranda of the manor house.

Long windows flanked by black shutters grace the elegant white facade, while twin chimneys rise from the roof toward the sky.

As a guest in this elegant mansion, the traveler may choose to stay in the suite which includes the former ballroom, or repose in the canopied queen bed of the Gun Room Suite. Guests can also choose whether they prefer a view of the rice fields or the avenue of oaks leading to the house.

Although other lodgers are probably fellow travelers spending a night or two, one lodger is here to stay. He has been here since antebellum times.

There is no existing document that mentions Peter Simon's property before 1794, but it has been estimated that the manor house which he built there may date as early as 1740.

When Peter Simon died in 1794, the executors of his will had a plot drawn up in order to divide the property evenly between his two sons, Peter, Jr., and John.

Peter, Jr., received the northern half of his father's property, a 966-acre tract of land stretching from the Waccamaw River to the Atlantic Ocean. This tract was called Willbrook.

John's inheritance was the southern half, a 966-acre tract reaching from the Waccamaw to the ocean. This tract, named Litchfield, included the existing manor house and the avenue of live oaks.

Sometime between November 1794 and 1796, John sold Litchfield to Daniel Tucker of Georgetown.

Daniel made full use of the Waccamaw River location of his new home, masterminding the creation of an intricate system of flooding and draining that was necessary for rice cultivation. This system used gates that opened from the river into a maze of narrow canals that ran through the rice fields.

Daniel did not have many years to enjoy the wealth earned from this great accomplishment. He died in 1797, leaving Litchfield to three of his six sons.

John Hyrne Tucker, the oldest of the three to inherit Litchfield, later became its sole owner. It is not known whether he made a financial arrangement with his brothers or simply outlived them.

During the course of his full and spirited life, John Hyrne Tucker perfected the rice-growing methods of his father. His devotion to rice planting escalated production on his land to a high point of one million pounds of rice in the year 1850.

In addition to rice planting, he was a devout Episcopalian, a noted connoisseur of fine wines, and president of a local social club that entertained, among other noted guests, former president Martin Van Buren.

Loved by all, John Hyrne Tucker married four times and fathered nine children.

Henry Massingberd Tucker, John Hyrne's son by his third wife, inherited Litchfield when his father died.

Realizing the tremendous responsibility handed down from his father and grandfather, Henry devoted his life to caring for Litchfield and those who lived there.

He studied to become a medical doctor so that he could meet the needs of his family and the hundreds of slaves on his plantation.

With a complete and highly skilled knowledge of the rice-planting industry, as well as competency in the medical profession, Dr. Tucker was in a position to run Litchfield smoothly. The good doctor became a pillar of strength to his relatives, friends, slaves, and acquaintances.

Although his initial reason for becoming a doctor was to fulfill the medical needs of his family and slaves, Dr. Tucker was unable to turn down anyone who needed medical attention. He was the closest doctor to all of the surrounding plantations, and, as a result, was often called out late at night for medical emergencies.

Dr. Tucker had the gates of Litchfield locked by his devoted old gatekeeper every night. Believing this servant had no relations in the world, the doctor considered him the best man for the job. The old servant lived close to the gatehouse. When the bell outside the gate was rung, his job was to come and open the gate.

Unbeknownst to Dr. Tucker, the aged gatekeeper had a young wife on a nearby plantation. He would often go and visit her at night, unaware that his master, tired and weary, might be locked out.

Arriving at the gate late at night, tired Dr. Tucker would rap on the bell with the metal base of his riding crop. Thinking that the old gatekeeper was merely asleep, he would rap harder and harder on the bell, until someone would finally come to open the gate. Sometimes, when no one on the grounds of the plantation heard the bell, he would tie up his horse, climb over the high fence, and wearily walk down the long avenue of oaks to his house.

Not wanting to wake up everyone in his household, Dr. Tucker would climb the back stairway to his room where he could finally get some rest.

The doctor was the last Tucker to own Litchfield. He died in 1904, having sold the plantation seven years earlier.

During his lifetime, Dr. Tucker's plantation truly was a small kingdom over which he, like his father and grandfather before him, was the conscientious and hard-working king. It is said that, because of his devotion to his beloved plantation, Dr. Tucker never really left his kingdom.

Later owners of Litchfield began to hear the bell beside the gate ring at night. When someone would go to answer the gate, no one could be found waiting there. People soon realized it was the ghost of Dr. Tucker ringing the bell. The bell finally was removed because the old doctor's ghost, although a welcome presence, beat so furiously on it that he caused the manor house occupants to lose a great deal of sleep.

Over the years, Dr. Tucker has been seen in his room on the second floor, as well as on the back stairway he used for his late night returns. Travelers unfamiliar with the good doctor and his habits could easily mistake him for a fellow guest.

Those choosing to dine in the elegant Carriage House Club, built over Dr. Tucker's original stables and carriage house, may also catch a glimpse of the good doctor as they enjoy the comforts and hospitality of his beloved kingdom built on rice.

The Litchfield Manor House is located
on Shell Road off of U.S. 17, approximately
13 miles north of Georgetown.

Alice

———— . . . ————

OF ALL THE GHOSTS in Georgetown County, perhaps the best known is Alice.

Many tales have immortalized the young girl whose spirit roams an old plantation house, searching for her lost ring.

Alice Belin Flagg, the only daughter of the family that owned the great Wachesaw Plantation, was groomed from birth to marry into another wealthy plantation family.

When Alice's father died, her older brother, Dr. Allard

Flagg, took over the responsibility of preparing his young sister for her future. The fact that Alice would marry one of her peers was never questioned. Georgetown County plantation princesses married plantation princes, period.

When the vivacious Alice fell in love, at the tender age of fifteen, with a handsome and successful young lumberman, her livid brother and acquiescent mother packed her off to a Charleston boarding school.

However, Alice's love had already given her an engagement ring. In order not to anger her family, she wore it on a ribbon around her neck and kept it hidden close to her heart.

Torn between respect for her family's wishes and her love for the lumberman, Alice dutifully accepted boarding-school life. She also participated in the social events, such as the annual St. Cecelia Ball, expected of a young lady of her class.

Alice knew that her mother and brother counted on the wealthy planters' progeny to lure her affections away from her beloved, but her love was true. She remained faithful to her beau, depending on thoughts of him to sustain her until boarding school was finished. Then she could go home and marry her true love.

The love in Alice's heart was not enough to keep her body strong for such a length of time. Weakened by despair and longing, she contracted a deadly fever.

Her brother, Allard, was summoned. He traveled to Charleston, and upon his arrival made immediate plans to take his sister back to the Hermitage, the Flaggs' creekside home at Murrells Inlet.

The journey was too long and arduous for the seriously ill Alice. She was comatose by the time Allard had her placed in her own bed at the Hermitage.

Alice was not aware that her physician brother, while examining her, discovered the ring she always wore around her neck.

She did not feel him petulantly snatch the ribbon and remove her ring. Neither did she know that he furiously threw the ring into the nearby creek.

Awakening briefly from her coma, feverish Alice automatically made the familiar gesture of placing her hand on the ring that rested over her heart.

The ring was not there to console her.

The last conscious moments of Alice's life were filled with bewilderment and distress, as she deliriously asked in vain for her ring.

After her death, Alice was temporarily laid to rest near the Hermitage.

When her mother, who had been visiting out of state, arrived home, a funeral was held for Alice at All Saints' Waccamaw Episcopal Church near Pawleys Island. Alice was permanently laid to rest in the churchyard there. Her grave was covered with a stone slab which says only "ALICE."

According to local tradition, Allard insisted that no other inscription than her first name commemorate his sister's grave. He felt that she disgraced the family unforgivably and did not deserve further acknowledgment.

Alice knew a life with her beloved would be difficult and hard-won, but she was fiercely determined to be with him always. Many believe that, even in death, Alice did not give up her hope of being united with her true love. In death, she continues to search for her ring, the symbol of her chosen man's affection.

Alice has been seen many times near her final resting place behind the wrought-iron gates of All Saint's Churchyard. Through the years, numerous guests at the Hermitage have also seen a vivid, life-like Alice standing in her old bedroom.

She is always wearing a long white dress, as if dressed for a wedding or burial. And always, always, she seems to be searching for her lost ring.

Alice's old home, the Hermitage, has been moved from its original creekside location in Murrells Inlet. It is no longer open to the public.

All Saints' Waccamaw Episcopal Church is located on Shell Road off of U.S. 17, approximately 12 miles north of Georgetown.

Hampton Plantation

——— . . . ———

IN ANTEBELLUM DAYS, many young couples were torn apart because of family disapproval. Alice Belin Flagg was not the only young romantic whose death was caused by a forbidden love.

Just as Alice's spirit haunts the Waccamaw Neck area where she loved, died, and was buried, the spirit of John Henry Rutledge lingers at the Hampton Plantation, his ancestral home near the South Santee River. He is forever grieving over a love that his family would not allow.

John Henry was one of eight children born during the early part of the nineteenth century to Hampton Plantation owners Frederick and Harriott Horry Rutledge.

John Henry knew that he was descended from a respected and historic line of French Huguenots. In fact, his family's very home, Hampton Plantation, was built in 1735 by the third-generation French Huguenot Noe Serré. John Henry's grandfather, Daniel, married Serré's daughter. She died childless, leaving Hampton to Daniel. He later married Harriott Pinkney, John Henry's grandmother.

John Henry's grandparents altered the original design of the mansion by adding a wide, sweeping front portico, completed not long before George Washington visited Hampton in 1791. Growing up, John Henry heard the glorious story many times of how his grandparents entertained the president of the nation at Hampton during their reign as governor and first lady of South Carolina.

He also was aware that his great-grandmother, Eliza Lucas, brought increased wealth to her family and other low country planters when she innovatively began growing indigo on the family plantation.

John Henry's parents went to great pains to instill responsibility and pride in their family heritage in their children. Harriott and Frederick Rutledge believed part of their duty included making sure that all their children married the progeny of equally illustrious families.

Thoroughly steeped in the glorious legacy of his family, John Henry felt a touch of pride every time he galloped down the wide expanse of grassy land that opened to reveal the magnificent facade of the Hampton mansion. He loved everything about his ancestral home—the dark-grey slate roof, the stately, white, unfluted columns on the wide front portico, and the graceful arches of the brick foundation.

But John Henry's life changed when he fell in love during his twenty-first year. He longed to bring his bride home to his beloved Hampton. But first he had to marry her, and that could be trouble. The young woman he loved was a proper lady in every way. She was well-educated and intelligent, as well as good-hearted and beautiful. Her voice, manners, and physical carriage were as elegant and refined as the most cultivated plantation belle. She would make a wonderful addition to the Rutledge family and a wonderful mother for the heirs to Hampton.

John Henry knew the only drawback was that his parents would object to the fact that she was the daughter of a pharmacist.

John Henry hoped his mother would understand, give her blessing, and convince John Henry's father to do the same. This could not have been further from what happened. Not only did the formidable Harriott Rutledge not understand, she was furious. She announced, in no uncertain terms, that John Henry could never marry a shopkeeper's daughter. Did he not realize, she said coldly, that he was a Rutledge?

John Henry was beside himself with frustration. He went upstairs and rocked dejectedly in his favorite chair by the open window. Why did the past, he thought sadly, have to determine his future?

Depressed and deep in thought, John Henry sat in his

favorite rocker as he tried to think of a solution. After several days he rode out of Hampton toward Georgetown, where the father of the girl he loved kept his shop.

John Henry told her father the sad story, holding nothing back. He poured out the truth about his love for the man's daughter, including his resolution to marry her at any cost.

No, the father stated adamantly. He would not allow his innocent daughter to marry into a family who considered her a lower class of person. It would be cruel, he said, to allow her to enter into a marriage under those conditions.

John Henry rode home feeling that all hope was lost.

Riding up to Hampton mansion, he felt tears sting his eyes as he visualized the girl he loved greeting him there. He imagined strolling through the back gardens to the creek behind the house, with his love, watching the flatboats being poled along toward the river.

John Henry retired to his bedroom, knowing he would find no solace there or anywhere else.

He rocked dejectedly in his chair, contemplating the rest of his life without the girl he loved.

On a fateful day in March 1830, while sitting in his rocker by the window, John Henry shot himself.

He did not die immediately. He lived on for two days, despite the fatal wound to his head. During this time he asked his family for forgiveness for his deed and bid a fond goodbye to them. He knew that they really loved him and that in their hearts they meant well.

John Henry died on March 30, 1830. He was buried in the back garden of Hampton, behind the mansion where he had lived and died.

Although his lifeless form has long been buried, the stain where the blood spilled from his wound onto the floor has come back countless times, despite sound scrubbings.

His spirit has been felt more often than seen in the upstairs bedroom where he died. His presence causes a dense, heavy feeling in the room.

His ghost is held responsible for the fact that the park superintendent often finds the alarm system turned off after he has turned it on.

The emotional turmoils John Henry experienced have left such an impression on Hampton Plantation they are still felt strongly today.

The centuries-old planks upstairs near the front window of John Henry's former bedroom seem to have absorbed the intense energy and despair of all he was feeling in March of 1830.

If you should choose to go upstairs into John Henry's bedroom at Hampton, perhaps you too will feel this energy.

Hampton Plantation State Park is located
off of U.S. 17, approximately 16 miles
south of Georgetown.

The Wedge

——— · · · ———

SEVERAL MILES southeast of Hampton Plantation lies the Wedge, another old rice plantation where past lives mingle with present ones. The Wedge plantation is nearly a century younger than its pre-Revolutionary neighbor, but it is every bit as haunted by its past.

The Wedge derived its name from the pie-shaped sweep of its grounds. The smallest point of this nineteenth-century rice domain is the front entrance area, which is just wide enough to accommodate its white wooden gate and posts. From here, the property fans out to include hushed woodlands, waterfowl-laden canals, and wide-open expanses of rice fields. These miles of fertile rice fields stretch far into the immense and breathtaking marshlands of the Santee Delta. Here the romantic, lonely moor-like scape stretches all the way to the horizon.

The Wedge plantation house was built in 1826 by South Carolina-born William Lucas. He was the youngest son of Jonathan Lucas, a celebrated Briton whose innovative creation of the water-powered rice-pounding mill greatly increased the Lucas family fortune.

William Lucas prospered as a second-generation rice baron, amassing five hundred slaves, an upstate summer home, a Charleston townhouse, and a four-thousand-acre estate on Murphy Island.

Among his many holdings, the Wedge plantation house was Lucas' *pièce de résistance*.

The house featured a brick foundation with many openings, so that air could flow through and keep moisture from settling. Rising from the graceful arches of this brick base, the house was designed as a classic example of Southern Greek Revival architecture.

It was formalized with stately, well-proportioned Doric columns. The severity of each column was softened by the placement of a Grecian-style wooden urn directly above it on the second-story piazza railing. William's elegant and subdued interpretation of Greek-Revival style has received much praise over the years for its proportion and modesty. The design of his plantation home did not fall prey to the construction of outsized columns or excessive porticos.

Set back amid enormous magnolias, gnarled nineteenth-century camellias, and moss-draped limbs of ancient oaks, the Wedge plantation house welcomed Lucas family members for over half a century.

Although the Wedge was his primary residence, William did not stay there during the tropically hot, hazy months when mosquitoes bred and flourished on the plantation.

The early nineteenth-century death rate from mosquito-borne malaria was quite high, and the mosquito population grew rampantly on the Santee Delta during the summer.

William vacated the Wedge early each spring, reputedly with greater haste than any of the nearby plantation gentry, for fear of the deadly fever.

One of William's contemporaries, the master of neighboring Harietta plantation, observed that the waters held behind the flood gates of the vast rice fields increased the mosquito population throughout the area. Essential to rice cultivation, this large-scale, forced containment of stagnant water provided the perfect breeding ground for the already prolific insects.

Ironically, Lucas' ancestral plantation home is now the International Center for Public Health Research, a University of South Carolina institute dedicated to the research and control of vector-borne diseases, particularly those carried by mosquitoes.

Although the practice of fleeing the delta during the summer months saved the Lucas family, death did come to the

plantation in the 1960s. It was then that the delta plantation was bought by Dr. Richard Baynard Dominick. It is
the ghost of Dr. Dominick that many believe haunts the
plantation today.

Dr. Dominick was known to be an intrepid safari
hunter. As a testimony to his passion for safari hunting,
Dr. Dominick filled the study of his laboratory with mounts
from some of the exotic wild game he stalked abroad.

Lining the study walls were heads of a chamois from the
Italian Alps, a Konzoni or Coke's hartebeest from Nairobi,
tommy gazelles from Kenya, and a water buffalo. Masks,
shields, and other native treasures shared the walls
with sepia-toned photographs of Dr. Dominick's roving
adventures.

One of the doctor's more sedate pursuits was collecting
moths and butterflies. A fellow of the Royal Entomological
Society of London, he had over thirty thousand mounts in
his collection.

Plagued in his later years by ill health, the formerly robust and active Dr. Dominick died on his beloved plantation. Although his death was officially attributed to a heart
attack, it is believed that Dr. Dominick hastened his de-
mise by using a cyanide-filled kill jar, commonly used by
entomologists for euthanizing moths and butterflies.

His remains were never removed from the Wedge. Dr.
Dominick's body was placed in a simple, wooden coffin and
buried in a grave on the plantation grounds. As he had
requested, there was no boundary or stone to distinguish

his final resting place from the surrounding countryside. Dr. Dominick is now and forever a part of the plantation he loved.

Mrs. Dominick continued to live at the Wedge until 1981. After her death the house was turned over to the University of South Carolina.

Now biologists carry out extensive insect research and experimentation at the Wedge. Graduate students also pursue their studies here, housed in modernized workers' cottages and in the plantation house itself.

When Dr. Dwight Williams first came to work at the Wedge, he stayed in the "Wedgeling," a former slave cottage.

Dr. Williams did not believe in ghosts, so he had no explanation for the constant presence of a large, black moth that accompanied him everywhere for his first three days.

"Wherever I was, it was," he said.

The insect's approximately four-inch wingspread made its presence quite obvious to Dr. Williams. However, the moth was slightly elusive. While it faithfully shadowed him everywhere he went, it never allowed him to get too close.

After the large, black moth followed Dr. Williams for three days, it disappeared.

Many who knew Dr. Dominick insisted that this was his inspection of Dr. Williams. After three days of following the new man around his old home and laboratory, watching his every move, Dr. Dominick was satisfied that this successor would do a good job.

Dr. Williams is not the only one on this old plantation to experience the presence of Dr. Dominick.

A former director of the Wedge had his office on the first floor of a two-story building which once served as the plantation manager's home.

One still, quiet afternoon, while working at his desk, the director heard an extremely loud noise on the second floor, directly above his head. This noise was followed by the unmistakable sound of a heavy object rolling across the floor.

He knew the ceilings were too high for the noise to come from something falling on the roof. He also knew he was alone in the building.

Rushing upstairs, the director searched the second floor and found absolutely nothing. Everything was in place, and nothing had fallen on the floor.

Could the loud sound have been Dr. Dominick asserting his presence?

Over the years, graduate students in residence at the Wedge have also experienced some eerie incidents.

One graduate student who was living in the main house had his books neatly organized on the shelves near his bed. Wedged between the books, and set back safely against the wall, was his portable radio. Alone in the upper section of the house, he turned on the radio and was enjoying the music played by a rock station. The student left the room briefly, leaving the radio playing.

When he returned to his room, the radio had been pushed off the shelf onto the floor. The surrounding books were undisturbed. No one had come into the upper portion of the house during his absence.

Another student awoke one night to the sound of some-one turning pages in a large book, such as an atlas. When he turned on a lamp and investigated there was no one nearby, nor was there a book large and heavy enough to make such a sound anywhere in the room.

Although outwardly serene and peaceful, the Wedge plantation is never truly at rest. The spirit of Dr. Dominick seems to wander the halls of his beautiful home with a watchful eye over those who come to stay here. Biologists continue their research of the various species of mosquito that regenerate so rapidly at the Wedge. As these scientific minds make advances against mosquito-carried illnesses and other vector-borne diseases, they are aware that they are not alone.

The Wedge is located beyond the turnoff
to Hampton Plantation State Park on U.S. 17.

Old Gunn Church

———— . . . ————

DRIVING DOWN the paved road that winds through the Pee Dee River portion of Georgetown County is like stepping back in time.

This area has a remote and mysterious air, heightened by the fact that one can drive for miles, through towering pines, without seeing another soul. Just off the road, in an area that is now completely isolated from human activity, an old church once stood that was the center of the plantation community. Although, only the foundation of the church and a lonely belltower still remain in this dark and desolate place, spirit voices can still be heard echoing from walls that crumbled long ago.

Along the road through this area are small, modest wooden signs that announce romantic-sounding names such as Nightingale Hall, Dirleton, Arundel, Chicora Wood, and Springfield. Each small sign marks the entrance to the plantation of a former Pee Dee River rice baron. Behind every name lies what was once a closely knit society of antebellum wealth. Most of these rice barons were Episcopalian, and the church played an important role in day-to-day life.

In the early eighteenth century, when the Pee Dee River area became established as an elite and thriving plantation community, Prince George, the Episcopal parish to which it belonged, divided.

The Pee Dee community became the center of the newly formed Prince Frederick parish. The Prince George parishoners built a new church in Georgetown, but the Prince Frederick congregation continued to worship at the old church on the Black River.

As the community grew, a new church for the Prince Frederick parish was begun in 1859 in the midst of their own spreading lands.

In mid-1860, progress on the new church's construction received a terrible blow. When Union ships blockaded Georgetown harbor, precious goods shipped from Europe for the church's completion were lost in the confusion.

Work on the church came to a complete halt later in 1860 when the head architect, Mr. Gunn, slipped on the high, incredibly steep roof and fell, screaming, to his death. The unfinished church, its massive bell tower rising above the tree tops, was temporarily abandoned.

Damage incurred during the war years added to the work that would be required to complete the structure.

In the decade after the Civil War, there wasn't enough money left in the once-prosperous community to complete construction of Prince Frederick's Church. However, donations from wealthy New York businessmen and other churches enabled work on the ill-fated church to conclude.

With their large and exquisite church completed, the planters of Prince Frederick parish now had a fine church of their own.

For a time, the church flourished. It was especially known for its choir of exceptionally talented voices. The choir, which practiced at dusk nearly every night, could be heard from miles around.

Sadly, though, the church soon fell on hard times. Antebellum days had ended, and poverty forced many formerly-rich rice planters to move away to find other ways of life and livelihood. The remaining parishioners could neither fill their lovely house of worship nor afford to keep it up. They were forced to move to a smaller, less beautiful, chapel.

For many years, Prince Frederick's was used on special occasions, such as Easter, and left unused the rest of the year.

The glorious choral voices no longer echoed through the forest.

Finally, services at Prince Frederick's Church, Pee Dee, were stopped altogether. The house of worship fell into a state of disrepair. In the last several decades, the remains were torn down after the main body burned.

All that remains now of the lovely gothic structure, begun in the age of opulence, are the ruins of the church foundation and the bell tower that still rises high into the sky above the towering pines.

Today this lonely keep, with only the ancient cemetery behind it, is the site of very strange and eerie occurrences.

Many believe that Mr. Gunn, the architect who tumbled to his death while building the church, still haunts the grounds. Gunn's spirit is said to be so prevalent in and around the tower that the belfry and church ruins have come to be known as the Old Gunn Church.

Georgetonians have told of seeing lights moving in the totally inaccessible upper portion of the tower during the night. Others have heard the bloodcurdling, horrible scream of Mr. Gunn, the architect, as he relives his fatal fall.

Mr. Gunn is not the only spirit that roams the grounds of the old church. The choir, that once resounded through the trees like a chorus of heavenly voices, still sings, although the choral members are all long gone. That magical time between sundown and dark, when their practice reached its crescendo, is exactly the time they are still ocassionally heard.

The choir's melodious voices are not loud. Rather they are unmistakably sweet, rising above and then blending into the wind as it sweeps through the tall surrounding pines.

The remains of Old Gunn Church
are located on SC 22-4 off of U.S. 701,
approximately 16 miles north of Georgetown.

Springfield

———— . . . ————

SPRINGFIELD PLANTATION, lying along the Pee Dee River, maintains its wide, impressive grounds, although the plantation house has long been gone.

The present owner's house is a modern dwelling, constructed in the same place where the manor once stood. The only remnant of the old house is a stone reminder of the front steps of the original plantation manor.

Near the manor house stands the white-frame cottage where the overseer lived alone except for the constant company of his two large and faithful dogs.

Although many thought the overseer was gruff and mean

because of his rough talk, those who truly knew him knew he was a kind man.

In his garden the overseer grew peas, potatoes, tomatoes, and many other delicious vegetables. He often invited people to harvest some of these vegetables for themselves. Then he would help them gather, making sure they got all they could carry.

The overseer rarely wore shoes in the warm months. This was an extremely risky habit at Springfield since poisonous rattlesnakes, known as "bell call" rattlesnakes because their rattlers were always up and ringing, were common in the area. Despite the apparent danger, this fearless man walked about Springfield barefoot even on the darkest nights, oblivious to the dangerous rattlesnakes that lurked in the paths surrounding the plantation.

In the deepest part of winter, the overseer was often alone at Springfield, save for his dogs. Cozy in his warm cottage, he saw no one for days at a time. His only company was a friend who lived on the central plantation road. This friend would travel down the long Springfield lane every few days to bring the overseer's mail.

One cold winter day, this friend was on his way with the mail. As he approached the overseer's home, he could not see the welcoming smoke that always rose from the overseer's cottage. This was odd, since the overseer always kept a fire going during the chilly weather.

Then the friend noticed something else. He saw one buzzard, then another, circling in the sky above the overseer's home. Fearing that something had happened to the man, his friend quickened his pace, hoping the buzzards were interested in something else. As he came closer to the house, his fears for the overseer heightened. The buzzards were circling directly over the cottage.

He leapt up the steps and rapped sharply on the front door, waiting only a moment before opening the door with a forceful thrust of his shoulder.

He walked into the house, dreading what he might find. A terrible sight lay before him.

The overseer's dogs, casting forlorn eyes at the friend, hovered over their master's dead body. With no one to feed them for days after their master's death, the desperately hungry dogs had eaten their beloved owner's head.

In the years after the overseer's death, Springfield visitors often described a mysterious man roaming about the plantation at night. The man was always accompanied by two large dogs. He wore no shoes. More horrifying to those who saw him, the mysterious man did not seem to have a head.

Through the years, many have beheld the overseer, roaming swiftly and unshod through the trees, past the dock and through the old slave cemetery, always in the company of two dogs and oblivious to the "bell call" of the wandering rattelsnakes.

Springfield Plantation is located
north of Georgetown on S.C. 22-4 off of U.S. 701.

Georgetown's National Register Historic District

Georgetown's National Register Historic District consists of an area five blocks deep by eight blocks wide, located adjacent to the Sampit riverfront.
This section of town was laid out by Elisha Screven in 1729, and now includes more than fifty historic sites, many of which are haunted.

The historic homes in this district are often referred to by two names. The first name is that of the builder, original owner, or earliest known owner, and the second is the name of the present owner.

For the purposes of this book, each is identified by the former name.

Henning House

——————— . . . ———————

OF THE MANY spirits that haunt Georgetown, none are known to be malicious or have ill intentions toward the living.

While all these spirits seem benign, only one is genuinely benevolent.

This kind spirit is the helpful ghost of Henning House. The circumstances that surround the spirit's inhabitation of the house were direct results of the British occupation of Georgetown during the Revolutionary War.

Located on the corner of Screven and Duke streets, the

Henning House was supposedly built around 1760. On the porch side, the house has the distinctive pre-Revolutionary architectural feature of nine-over-nine sash windows—window frames that have nine panes of glass in each sash, both upper and lower halves. This porch side faces quiet Screven Street.

In colonial homes, the owners often extended the house wall to the end of the porch for privacy. Colonists loved to entertain on their spacious, breezy piazzas, but did not necessarily want to be seen by prying eyes.

The Henning House has such a wall facing busy Duke Street. To insure further privacy, but still allow access to the piazza from Duke Street, a door was built in the flat sheer wall along the busy street. When you open this door, you have to climb a staircase before reaching the porch. From most angles on Duke Street, passersby cannot get a good look at, or from many angles even see, the Henning House piazza.

Since the 1760s, many individuals have passed through the quaint privacy door of the Henning House. During the 1770s, quite a few of these guests were British soldiers.

. . .

During the Revolutionary War, most of the people of Georgetown were Patriots. One of their greatest local heroes was Francis Marion, the notorious general known as the Swamp Fox.

A gracious gentleman who grew up in the South Carolina low country, Francis Marion hunted and fished the vast swamps and dark rivers of southeastern Carolina all his life. He was just as comfortable in the cavernous green labyrinths of a cypress swamp as he was in the drawing room of an elegant townhouse in Georgetown or Charleston.

In the seclusion of his camp, deep in the brush of Snow Island at the mouths of the Great and Little Pee Dee rivers, the Swamp Fox planned intricate strategies to confound the British.

His greatest tactic, from which his nickname was derived, was allowing the British to chase him deep into the murky mazes of the coastal Carolina swamps. Using his vast knowledge of the area, the Swamp Fox, would slip away undetected, leaving the British soldiers to flounder helplessly until they eventually found their way out of the maze-like mire.

For this reason particularly, the British militia detested Francis Marion. Every soldier serving under the British Crown on South Carolina soil knew that the capture of the Swamp Fox would be a grand coup.

Most of the citizens of Georgetown supported the Patriot cause, but some were British sympathizers. Though few in number, these sympathizers, known as Tories, were staunch in their loyalty to the King. Some even allowed British soldiers to stay in their homes. Usually, when the British militia needed quarters, they simply took over the home of a Patriot. However, they didn't enjoy the same hospitality in a Patriot's home as they did in the home of a Tory. To have graciously appointed quarters and fine dining offered by a family allegiant to the Crown was a rare treat for the soldiers.

One such hospitable British sympathizer was the owner of the Henning House.

This gentleman and his daughter opened their spacious upstairs guest quarters to several young soldiers of the Crown. These fortunate British lads were grateful for the comfortable beds and friendly atmosphere of the Henning House.

It was relaxing to be able to come home and discuss military strategies in the bosom of a Tory household rather than in a Patriot dwelling, where they would have to watch their tongues.

Unbeknownst to the owner of the Henning House or his military guests, the daughter of the home was, in fact, a Patriot sympathizer.

None of the British soldiers had any qualms about discussing top-secret military business in front of the young lady. How aghast they would have been had they known she was documenting their important conversations and passing the information to the Swamp Fox!

Although the young woman had kept her devotion to the Patriot cause hidden from her father, she was determined to aid the Patriots in any way she could. Whenever she heard British plans being discussed, she would steal away under cover of night and relay them to Marion.

Marion was able to use the information the young woman gave him to strike several blows at the British. The British militia occupying Georgetown became more and more frustrated as Francis Marion continuously foiled their operations in the area. The Swamp Fox actually seemed to anticipate their carefully laid plans.

The British soldiers occupying Georgetown constantly lived in this heightened state of frustration, literally flinching in anger when the name "Francis Marion" was mentioned.

One afternoon, a young British officer was resting in his quarters upstairs in the Henning House.

He and several of his men had spent an exhausting night chasing the phantasmagorical Swamp Fox. They had traveled countless miles through a horrible swamp muck on the Waccamaw Neck, only to find that their quarry had disappeared.

The exhausted officer was deep in slumber when he heard a great commotion downstairs.

He started, torn between sleep and wakefulness. Then a few excited words caught his attention.

". . . just spotted the Swamp Fox in Georgetown."

This brought the officer instantly to his feet. In seconds, the young officer was up and into his breeches and high boots.

He was hastily buttoning his shirt, jacket tucked under his arm, when he rounded the corner at the top of the stairs and began his downward dash.

In his mad rush, he forgot a structural flaw near the top of the stairs.

The officer always climbed up and down the stairs with extreme caution because of an uneven riser near the top of the flight. He knew a nasty fall would result if he did not tread carefully on this plank.

In his excitement over the elusive Swamp Fox's alleged proximity, the young soldier forgot all about the uneven riser. He tripped on it and fell headlong to the bottom of the stairs.

The young officer lay hopelessly still when his fall ended.

Only after a doctor pronounced the man dead of a broken neck did his comrades sadly straighten his crumpled form and close his sightless eyes.

The British militia occupying Henning House grieved deeply over the loss of their young comrade, and, for a time, they forgot all about pursuit of their fox-like nemesis.

After the Revolutionary War ended and the British soldiers returned home, an unusual presence was noticed at the Henning House.

Although the unfortunate British officer was the only person to ever fall to his death on the uneven riser, he was by no means the only person to stumble on it. After the young officer's tragic accident, anyone who tripped on the uneven riser was instantly caught by a strong and gentle arm. The distinctly human-like force would then steady the rescued person before letting go.

In the more than two hundred years since the British

officer's death, a number of people have tripped on the uneven riser near the top of the central staircase of the Henning House. However, they all have been saved by the benevolent spirit of the young British officer. To this day, he guards the house to make sure no one else meets a sad fate similar to his.

The Henning House, built circa 1760,
is located at 331 Screven Street at
the corner of Duke Street.

Heriot House

———— . . . ————

ON THE BLUFF above the last bend before the Sampit River opens into Winyah Bay, sits the graceful and charming Heriot House.

Built around 1760 at the river end of Cannon Street, this stately dwelling commands a breathtaking view of the Georgetown waterfront from its high perch.

The Heriot House has been the scene of such intense romance and intrigue through the years that those involved have left indelible impressions upon the house. All of the clandestine events that have so affected this dwelling have been direct results of the home's key position above the river.

The builder of the Heriot House is not known, but it is obvious that he took great care to keep the construction of the house appropriate to its glorious location.

The brick foundation of the house was designed with a series of high arches. These vaulted crescents not only lent beauty to an otherwise plain portion of colonial construction, they also provided ventilation for the lower floor. This feature has proved invaluable in saving the Heriot House from the occasional flooding and constant dampness brought by close proximity to the river.

The generous area under the foundation created a cool cellar where residents stored fruits and vegetables during the subtropical summer months.

Along the bottom of each long plank of the home's clapboard siding is a carved, horizontal bead. This edge, a common feature of the time, was meant to act as a rain repellant. It forced the rain to the right or left of each clapboard rather than letting the liquid seep into the wood. The beaded edge along the clapboard siding has been a major factor in preserving the exterior of this home despite its exposure to bitter storms that sweep in from the Atlantic.

Adding to the quintessentially colonial style of the Heriot House are the nine-over-nine sash windows, many panes of which still contain hand-blown glass. The glass is identifiable by its tell tale bubbles and wavy countenance.

A massive king post, which can be seen emerging from

the striking red-tiled roof, runs squarely through the center of the structure. This huge central support provides a uniquely ship-like central stability to the house, comparable to that of the tall-masted sailing vessels that docked nearby.

An early owner of the Heriot House built two red-brick buildings directly across Cannon Street from his home. One was a waterfront warehouse called the Red Store. The other was a three-story tavern called the French Tavern or the Oak Tavern.

The warehouse was used to store mail, silks, French wines, and other imported rarities that were unloaded from the huge sailing ships docked at the adjacent Red Store wharf. Many travelers also boarded and disembarked from ships at the Red Store wharf. The area across the street from the Heriot House became the scene of many joyous reunions and tearful goodbyes. Those who set sail from the Red Store wharf faced their journey with a mixture of excitement and apprehension, for sea travel was still dangerous in those days. Many of the travelers on these sailing vessels never reached their destination.

On the night of December 30, during the War of 1812, the packet ship *Patriot* was tied up at the Red Store wharf, awaiting its cargo and passengers.

The *Patriot* was sailing for New York the next day. Among her booked passengers was the glamorous Theodosia Burr Alston, wife of South Carolina Governor Joseph Alston and daughter of the former vice-president, Aaron Burr.

On the eve of her journey, Theodosia was entertained in a nearby townhouse where friends were giving a farewell fete in her honor.

The soirée ended early, and Theodosia returned to her comfortable lodgings at the Heriot House, where she was to spend the night before her voyage.

On the morning of December 31, Theodosia walked down the Red Store wharf and boarded the *Patriot*. She expected to spend a fortnight at sea—perhaps less if the weather was favorable.

Sad and disconsolate, the normally dynamic young woman did not care if the journey took months, except that she longed to see her father in New York. Theodosia had been slow to recover her natural gaiety, lively spirits, and fair health following the death of her only son the previous summer. Adding to her poor condition was a recent bout with ill health, as well as constant worry for her father.

Aaron Burr had been known as one of America's greatest statesmen when he served as Thomas Jefferson's vice-president. However, Burr was known for his fiery temper, which had recently caused him a great deal of trouble. Not only was he accused of treason for plotting against the United States, he had also killed Alexander Hamilton, the former Secretary of the Treasury, in a duel.

It was hoped by Theodosia, and all who loved her, that the ocean voyage to New York and the extended visit with her father might restore her health and spirits.

After the *Patriot*, with Theodosia aboard, sailed into the brisk Atlantic, neither the ship nor her passengers were ever seen or heard from again.

It is believed that the *Patriot* was caught in a fierce January storm and sank after foundering on the deadly rocks off the treacherous Outer Banks of North Carolina. Others speculate that the vessel's heavy guns, a necessary precaution during the War of 1812, broke from their mounts during a storm and gouged the *Patriot*'s hull, causing her to break up and sink.

More eerily, there are tales of deathbed confessions from pirates who swore with their dying breaths that they had captured the *Patriot* and murdered all on board.

Whatever the fate of the lovely Theodosia, she took her last footsteps on earth in front of the Red Store beside the Heriot House.

She is rumored to still linger along the waterfront by the Heriot House. It is said that she comes there to eternally retrace the footsteps of her last moments on earth, before the sailing vessel *Patriot* carried her to her death.

. . .

Many believe the spirit of another beautiful young woman also roams the grounds around the Heriot House.

Several years after the death of Theodosia, in the era of wealth and opulence that preceded the Civil War, a lovely, golden-haired girl lived with her parents in the already historic Heriot House.

She was a well-educated, sheltered Georgetown belle whose favorite pastime was caring for her dogs.

One afternoon, this sweet-natured girl was strolling along the waterfront near her home with her two immaculately groomed canines. Her beauty and grace caught the attention of a handsome young man who was aboard one of the ships docked at her father's wharf.

The young Northern man, a crew member of his uncle's great sailing ship, had never seen a woman as breathtaking as the elegant figure who meandered along the riverside, her parasol in one hand and the dual leash of her proper, well-mannered dogs in the other.

The smitten young gallant wasted no time in making the acquaintance of the pretty girl, much to her delight.

The two had an instant rapport. They began to rendezvous daily during the hour the young lady walked her dogs.

When the girl's father discovered his daughter had a beau off a Yankee ship, he furiously told the captain to keep his nephew away from the girl or dock his ship somewhere else.

The ship's captain chose to dock elsewhere rather than meddle in his nephew's love life.

To the dismay of the young belle and her beau, the ship was forced to anchor out in the harbor, as no other tie-up was available along the busy waterfront at that time.

Love, however, quickly and ingeniously found a way.

The determined and innovative young Northerner immediately sent his belle a message. He told her to signal when her parents were asleep by placing a light in the third-story dormer window of her home. Then he would know that she could safely slip out of the house, and he could come from the ship to meet her.

The girl eagerly complied, delighted that her romance was not foiled after all. From the lofty window she could see far across Winyah Bay. The young man would have no trouble seeing her light from aboard the ship's lonely anchorage.

That very night, the young couple began using their signal to meet in the formal, bay laurel maze beside the Heriot House. Here, among the dense ornamental hedges, the young couple would stroll hand in hand and embrace without fear of discovery.

Resigned to follow a secret relationship, the handsome Northern man and the Georgetown belle parted with plans to meet whenever the young man's ship was in the vicinity.

For nearly twenty years, the golden-haired lady placed a light in the appointed window late at night to signal her beau whenever his ship docked in the Georgetown harbor. They continued to rendezvous in the quiet of the bay laurel maze but never married, even after parental consent was no longer a factor.

For reasons unknown, the Northern man eventually stopped coming. He visited neither Georgetown nor the lady. It is not known what fate befell him; whether he married another, died, or simply ended the relationship. Whatever the reason, the lady became bitter and reclusive. Her memories of their stolen moments haunted her.

She continued to place the light in the window, but did

so less and less. Each time she lit the little flame that once heralded her sweet, clandestine meeting, she gazed across the harbor, wondering what had become of her lover.

Often, very late at night, the lonely lady would walk her dogs in the old maze. Even as she felt the bitter winter winds that whistled through the branches she remembered the warm nights filled with the scent of bay laurel.

The beloved dogs of her girlhood had given way to a pack of faithful dogs. These canines were their mistress' only companions as well as her protectors. The dogs made her feel safe even though she was all alone in the big waterfront house.

Even during the darkest days of the Civil War, when Union ships and gunboats blockaded the harbor, she felt secure due to her devoted and formidable canine friends.

As those wronged or disappointed in love often do, the lady turned her attention from her grief to a greater cause.

The Union blockade of Georgetown's harbor had deprived the Confederate troops of desperately needed medical supplies.

The watchful lady of the Heriot House began placing a light in the uppermost window to signal blockade runners that all was clear. When the blockade runners saw this signal they knew they could slip into the harbor undetected by Union ships and unload their precious, life-saving supplies.

The lady of the Heriot House saved many lives by using her vantage point high over the harbor to covertly help the Confederate smugglers.

After the war was over, the lady grew more and more reclusive. Once again, she rarely spent time with any companions save her faithful dogs. Naturally, much good-natured barking emitted from the home of the pack of pampered canines.

For this reason, no one paid much attention to the howling that resounded through the house one moonlit night, even though the sound carried eerily throughout the neighborhood.

The dogs often bayed at the moon when it was full, as it was that evening. However, as the night wore on, the howling did not stop. By morning it had reached a terrible crescendo.

Neighbors, worried about the reclusive lady, were unable to get her to answer her door. Finally, around mid-morning, they broke in to see if she was hurt or ill.

A large dog met the well-meaning intruders at the door. Alternately growling and whining, it scarcely allowed them to cautiously make their way toward the sound of the eerie howling.

Once past the large dog the neighbors quickly found out why the pack of canines had been baying so mournfully the whole night.

The mistress of Heriot House lay dead on the floor.

Over half a dozen howling dogs, both large and small, guarded the body of their dead mistress.

Nearby was a bucket of water with a dipper laying beside it. Those who found her assumed that the lady died while fetching water for her canine friends.

After the lady's death, strange events began to occur around the house.

At first, the next occupants of Heriot House were baffled by a light shining beneath the door of the rarely used third-floor dormer room. The source of the light was never discovered and, as time passed, they became used to it.

What they never grew accustomed to was something more discreet, but much more unsettling—the faint sound of dogs' nails clicking across the hardwood floors.

Strange lights and sounds aside, the Heriot House was a happy home to more than one owner until shortly after the turn of the century. Then the house was vacated. Soon the charming old home, neglected and unloved, became a haven for vagrants and hobos. During Prohibition, rumrunners placed lights in the uppermost window of the dark, nearly deserted, Heriot House to signal their companions in the harbor that it was safe to bring their illegal cargo into town for unloading.

Lights, both real and ghostly, were often seen in the high dormer window of the old home.

Nearby residents spoke in hushed tones of seeing a mysterious young couple walking among the overgrown bay laurels that were once clipped and trained into a formal maze.

Always, too, there was an eerie howling that came from the house on nights of the full moon.

During the late 1930s, the Heriot House was bought and restored to its former beauty. After the restoration, whisperings of strange occurrences decreased, but did not stop.

Even now, when the moon is full and high over Georgetown harbor, a light is sometimes seen in the third-story window of the Heriot House, and a golden-haired girl may be glimpsed near the waterfront, strolling with her secret lover.

The Heriot House, built circa 1760,
is located at 15 Cannon Street on the
Georgetown waterfront.

Waterman House

———— · · · ————

ONE OF THE MOST natural tendencies in the world is to seek the familiar.

A spirit will often linger close to its earthly home, finding comfort in the intimate surroundings, even though the last interval of life may have been unhappy.

Such is the case of the two spirits that haunt the Waterman House.

Built around 1770 on Highmarket Street, this elegant and dignified old dwelling was constructed in the typical pre-Revolutionary Georgetown style. The house is situated close to the road. The street frontage of the home is only one room wide, but the side of the house perpendicular to the street is much wider, extending far back onto the property and bordered by a long piazza.

It has been suggested that homes were constructed in this manner so that every room could take advantage of the refreshing breezes from the river. However, only the very narrow side of the Waterman House faces the waterfront. Instead, the house was situated this way because a tax law of that period stated that property was taxed according to its street frontage only. Builders of the time placed the smallest side of the house facing the street in order to avoid the higher taxes.

During the two centuries since it was built, the Waterman House has seen the transition from the era of graceful wooden sailing vessels to modern steel-hulled ships.

Back in the days when tall-masted ships sailed in and out of Georgetown harbor, bringing foreign goods into port and departing with cargoes of rice and indigo, a beautiful young lady lived with her parents in the Waterman House.

Her mind was constantly on the ocean and the harbor, for her beau was a wild and restless sea captain.

The young lady's parents vehemently disapproved of the match. Their daughter's beloved was also a cousin, a relationship that in those days usually warranted parental approval as it kept inheritances in the same families. However, these parents knew that the captain had a reputation for being a faithless suitor. The parents often tried to warn their daughter about him, but these warnings went unheeded by the determined young lady.

From her upstairs dormer window, the girl could see the wharves of the busy port. She often looked over the roofs of the nearby homes and riverfront taverns to the docks along the Sampit River, where her captain tied his dinghy after leaving his ship at anchor in the harbor.

She always knew when her lover departed, but even he could not name the date he would return, for ocean travel was dependent on the whims of the wind and the weather.

Early one afternoon, the captain strode purposefully up the steps of his love's Highmarket Street home.

He had just returned from a very lengthy, but highly successful, voyage to a foreign land. He was so anxious to see the beautiful young maiden he had barely taken time to tie up his dinghy after rowing to town from his ship's anchorage.

Avoiding the disapproval in her parent's eyes, the young lady barely hid her excitement as she greeted her captain. She noted the salt spray on his handsome face and the package in his hands.

Keeping a discreet distance from each other, the pair walked hand in hand in the formal garden behind the house, daring to steal a kiss only after twilight began to fall.

Later, as they sat on the piazza in the near-darkness, the captain gave the young lady the package he was carrying.

Her eyes grew wide as she drew out a bottle that glistened in the early moonlight.

The exquisite little vial contained a rare and exotic perfume she had only read about, never dreaming she would be given some for her very own. She knew its strong scent was intoxicating. The young lady squealed in delight as she dabbed a tiny bit of the perfume on her neck. The captain was pleased that she was so fond of the gift, but he gravely warned her never to put the perfume to her lips. If ingested, he cautioned, the perfume was a deadly poison.

The hour grew late, and the captain gave the young lady a lingering good night kiss as they stood on the dark piazza.

The young lady went into the house and closed the door behind her. Holding her flowing skirts with one hand and her gift of precious perfume in the other, she climbed to the third floor.

From the dormer window of her favorite treetop room, she stood watching her captain walk down the darkened streets. She occasionally lost sight of him as he passed by other tall houses but followed his path until he was close to the river. Dreading the moment when she would lose sight of him, the young lady was surprised to see that the captain went not to his dinghy but to a riverside tavern.

Framed in the moonlight by the dormer casement, she pondered her lover's actions. He had mentioned being tired and had told her he was going directly to his ship to go to sleep. Curious, the young lady kept a vigil by the window, her eyes fixed on the tavern door for what seemed like hours.

Looking down at the watch around her neck, she saw that not even a full half hour had passed since her captain had gone inside the tavern.

Raising her head again, she saw him coming out of the tavern with his arm around the shoulders of a local wench.

Shocked and horrified, the young lady stepped back from the window. A sinking, unreal feeling came over her. All his promises, all his words of love, all had been lies!

She continued to watch the pair as they headed down the street, hoping that what she was seeing was simply a cruel trick of her imagination. When the pair entered the door of a local inn, she knew that what she was seeing was real.

A great and violent despair overtook her. After all her waiting, loving, and longing, her faithless lover had proven her parents right after all. At once she knew that she could never see the captain again, nor could she ever love another.

The sparkling vial of deadly perfume on her dresser caught her eye. As she picked it up, it became clear to her what she must do. She opened the bottle and gulped down the vile, sweet-smelling liquid.

Death came swiftly and cruelly to the young lady.

Later that night, unable to row all the way out to his ship due to the very low tide, the captain returned to town and walked to the girl's home. The unusually low tide was an excellent opportunity for him to see his true love once again before sailing out of Georgetown harbor. No time spent with another woman ever quenched his desire to steal a kiss from his trusting beloved's innocent lips.

Upon arriving at the young lady's home, the captain was shocked to learn of her death. His shock turned to horror as he realized she had drunk the poisoned perfume.

The girl's spirit has never left her old home. She still keeps a vigil in the dormer window of her favorite treetop room, waiting and watching for her faithless captain.

. . .

The beautiful young lady by the window is not the only spirit in the Waterman House. Like several of Georgetown's haunted homes, the Waterman House is inhabited by a second spirit. This spirit belongs to a young boy whose grief for his missing family caused his early death.

During the early part of the nineteenth century, there was a wealthy family that lived on their Sampit River plantation during the cool part of the year and resided at their seaside home a few miles north of the plantation during the summer. This was a large and happy family with many children, the youngest of which was an eight-year-old boy.

The little boy loved to visit the Waterman House, which his family also owned. It was the home of his dear and best friend, a little girl just his age. The girl's father was a distant relative of the boy's family, as well as their lawyer, and the family was pleased for him to make their townhouse his home.

As summer approached one year, the family decided to take an ocean voyage to New England and stay at the seashore there instead of summering at their seaside home. They made plans to stay at one of New England's posh resorts and to visit Boston and New York.

Almost everyone in the family was excited about the trip,

particularly the oldest son. After the summer was over he would stay in New England as a student at one of the great universities there. The only person who was not pleased with the plans was the youngest boy. The idea of a long summer trip did not appeal to him at all. His entire summer would pass without one visit to see his best friend in Georgetown.

When the news of the little boy's feelings reached the Waterman House, the girl's father decided to ask if the child could stay in Georgetown for the summer. The man knew that his little girl would face a lonely summer without her favorite young friend, and he enjoyed the boy's company in a fatherly, caring way.

The boy's father agreed and the little boy was able to enjoy the festive revelry that surrounded his family's departure because his family was allowing him to spend the summer with his best friend and her father in Georgetown.

He happily waved goodbye to his family from the lawyer's little sailboat in Winyah Bay. He delightedly called out to his parents, brothers, and sisters as they stood behind the rail of the great swift sailing ship that was rapidly taking them out into the Atlantic.

As the lawyer's little craft made its way into Georgetown, the boy looked at his friend and her father, imagining what a happy summer the three of them would have together. He could not have guessed what his summer would hold.

A few days after the little boy's family began their journey, the ship was sailing off the Outer Banks of North Carolina when it was overcome by a storm of tremendous proportions. The great wooden sailing vessel was not able to steer away from the deadly rocks. No one aboard lived through the storm.

The little boy was resigned to not seeing his family for several months so the full magnitude of their fate did not strike him when he was initially told of the terrible accident. As he gradually began to realize that he would never see his family again, he became increasingly anxious about his family's death.

He worried endlessly over the fate of his mother and father. He thought of how his brothers and sisters must have struggled before they perished. He could hardly believe he would never be able to spend time with any of them again.

Soon the once-happy little boy became miserable. He was terribly nervous and unable to concentrate on anything but the awful fate of his family. He cried easily and often, spending hours alone in his room, rocking disconsolately in the old chair by the window. His voracious appetite and playful nature dwindled away. He became thin and pale.

The doctors chosen by the lawyer to examine the little boy explained that the child was suffering from depression and shock as a result of losing his whole family at once. Love, care, understanding, and time were the only treatments that any of these physicians had to offer. The lawyer and his little girl lavished affection on the heartbroken child, knowing that their kind patience was the best medicine for him.

Gradually, the sad, withdrawn little boy began to recover his cheerful and relaxed disposition. A pleasant-natured child since birth, he found more reasons to smile as the months passed. Old interests began to tug at his attention. He delighted in accompanying the lawyer on hunting and fishing trips. Day sailing trips with the lawyer and the little girl were also a favorite activity for the little boy.

The only inhibiting aspect of the boy's recovery was his health. Although he had increased in height since the tragedy, his full weight never returned. His appetite was normal for a young boy, but he never regained his robust health.

Colds and fevers plagued the little boy. His body seemed to have little resistance to infection, and each bout of illness seemed to last longer than the one before it.

While recovering from a particularly bad chest cold, the child suddenly developed an alarmingly high fever. The lawyer immediately recognized that this illness was much more dangerous than any the boy had experienced before.

None of the doctors summoned by the worried lawyer were able to lower the child's high temperature or calm the feverish energy that consumed him.

The fever made the boy delirious and seemed to renew the distress and anguish that had tormented him following the deaths of his family. Despite efforts to keep him in the bed, he constantly left his bed to sit in his chair by the window, rocking and wringing his hands. Incessantly, he spoke of his brothers and sisters, repeating their names over and over. Aloud, he brooded over the fate of his parents. His high fever caused him to soak a fresh, white cotton nightgown every few hours. He hardly slept at all, unable to fall into any but the most fitful, nightmare-wracked slumber.

As the child withdrew deeper into his delirium, he took less notice of the real world around him. He seemed unaware of the loving hands that bathed his burning skin and changed his damp nightgowns for crisp, dry ones. Twisting his hands in agitation, he was conscious only of the awful deaths his family must have suffered in the shipwreck. The names of his brothers and sisters were constantly on the suffering child's lips. Several days after his fever had begun, death brought him peace.

The lawyer and the little girl were heartsick. There was no way to fill the emptiness that their small friend's death had left in their home and their affections.

More than a month after the little boy's passing, a servant came rushing down the stairs from the second-floor bedrooms. She swore in terror that she had seen the child sitting in the rocking chair by the window in his room. Nothing could convince her to return to the room that day. Only a thorough examination of the room by the lawyer convinced her to resume her upstairs duties later in the week.

The lawyer's little girl, hearing of the servant's experience, began to watch the little boy's bedroom often. She missed her treasured friend and hoped to catch a glimpse of him.

Days passed and the little girl neither saw nor heard anything unusual in her companion's room. She continued to
linger hopefully in the doorway dozens of times a day, staring wistfully at the old rocker where her playmate had spent
so many hours.

One evening, just before her bedtime, the little girl stole
to her old friend's doorway for one last look before retiring.

Silhouetted against the moonlit window of his room sat
the sad little boy, rocking in his old wooden chair. He was
dressed in a spotless white gown made iridescent by the
bright moonlight. Wringing his pale hands and whimper-
ing softly, he seemed unaware of the little girl's audible gasp.

She rushed forward in anxious delight to greet her beloved friend. She wanted to embrace him and comfort him,
but the small figure disappeared just as she reached the
chair. She was left alone in the room, gazing at the still-
moving rocker.

Over the years, the girl saw her old playmate many more
times, but she was never able to get close enough to talk to
him before he disappeared.

Overnight guests in the Waterman House, unaware of
the sad story of the little boy, would ask about the little
boy they saw crying upstairs. No one has ever been able to
get close enough to comfort him.

. . .

Both the young woman whose unfaithful suitor drove her
to suicide and the little boy continue to reside in the
Waterman House today. Sitting beside their respective

windows, each one continues to stare longingly toward the ocean, eternally grieving over what they lost so many years ago.

The Waterman House, built circa 1770,
is located at 622 Highmarket Street.

Pyatt House

———— . . . ————

BESIDE THE STATELY Waterman House stands the Pyatt House, where the spirit of another child haunts the room where he died. However, this child is not the only spirit who resides at the Pyatt House. The house is also home to ghostly pranksters who delight in playing jokes on visitors.

The Pyatt House was built some thirty years after the Waterman House, during the years when colonial architecture was still the style of choice for most rice planters' homes in Georgetown. However, the Pyatt House is strikingly different from the majority of Georgetown's homes built in this era.

Although the Pyatt House was designed with the typical eighteenth-century details of clapboard siding with a beaded edge and nine-over-nine sash windows, the arresting feature of the house is that the widest side directly faces Highmarket Street. This makes the house noticeably different from most other eighteenth-century homes whose narrowest side faces the street.

Another distinguishable feature is the high piazza which offers a view of well-traveled Highmarket Street. This front veranda is built a full story above the ground in the West Indies style, forming a complete bottom story where house slaves once lived. Most eighteenth-century Georgetonian homes were built with a much lower piazza entrance. In these homes, slave quarters were generally located on the third story.

The ground floor of the Pyatt House is fronted by a pale-pink stone facade, arching around brick fretwork. The confection-colored stone is naturally pink coral rock, also called Bermuda stone because it was brought to Georgetown from Bermuda.

Two sets of brick steps, fronted by pastel pink stucco, lead up to the entrance from opposite sides. This masonry style is markedly different from any other structure in the historic district.

It has been suggested that, as in the case of certain antebellum Charleston homes, there were two sets of steps leading to the piazza so ladies and gentlemen could ascend from opposite sides. In this way, a lady could climb the steps to reach the gracious gathering above without the discomfort

of wondering if gentleman planters were mischievously eye-
ing her from below.

The Pyatt House, now owned by John and Patricia
Wylie, is run as the 1790 Bed and Breakfast and is still the
scene of genteel hospitality.

The Wylies' most requested accomodation, the Rice
Planter's Room, was supposedly haunted by the spirit of a
sick baby that died there over a century ago. For years
after the infant's death, owners, as well as visitors to the
home, were surprised by the sight of a mysterious woman
rocking a baby. Even when the woman and baby did not
appear, any rocking chair placed in the room would soon
begin to rock on its own.

The Rice Planter's Room has been elegantly restored by
the Wylies. It is dominated by a high step-up rice planter's
bed and graced by a sofa-sized window seat. However, it
pointedly does not have, among its exquisite and relaxing
furnishings, a rocking chair. So far, none of the Wylies'
guests have mentioned any ghosts in the Rice Planter's
Room, and the genial proprietors have no plans to test the
spirits of the woman and baby by placing a rocking chair
there.

. . .

Although the mysterious woman and child have not appeared in the Rice Planter's Room for some time, many of
the Wylies' overnight guests have experienced strange
occurrences in other parts of the house.

One guest staying alone in the room named Gabrielle's

Library was awakened during the night by the sound of his camcorder. He got out of bed, turned it off, and went back to bed a bit puzzled. He assumed he must have left the machine on, although he usually did not overlook such important details.

Later in the night, the gentleman was awakened again by the camcorder's distinctive hum. Scarcely able to believe what he was hearing, he got up to examine the camera and found it running again.

At breakfast the following morning, his first question to the Wylies was, "Do you have ghosts?"

This was not the first occasion something inexplicable happened in the Pyatt House, nor the only time a guest had asked the Wylies this question. John and Patricia Wylie have heard mysterious noises since they bought the house in 1992. Some of these sounds simply can not be attributed to the characteristic settlings of a large old house.

One afternoon, not long after moving in, John was working alone on the ground floor of the house. Suddenly he heard the unmistakable sound of feet running on the floor above. He searched the upper floors, only to confirm that all was secure. No one was anywhere to be found in the house, nor could anyone have entered through the locked doors.

A couple staying in the Prince George Suite, the lodgings in the dormer area of the Pyatt House, awoke in the night to find their bed rocking.

The man and woman were quite surprised but not frightened. Surely, they thought, there was a sensible explanation. They quickly went back to sleep.

Suddenly, they were again awakened by the vigorous rocking of the bed.

The next morning, the couple was eager to ask their hosts the inevitable question, "Do you have ghosts?"

"Yes," the Wylies answered, as they do each time the question is asked, "we do have ghosts."

After many strange and inexplicable occurrences, the Wylies tried to contact previous inhabitants of the house to see if they had similar experiences. A long chat with two women who had spent their girlhood in the Pyatt House confirmed that spirits were often present there.

The sisters were the first to tell the Wylies the legend of the rocking chair in the Rice Planter's Room.

The sisters were unable to explain the other ghosts in the Pyatt House, but they did reminisce about the regularity of phantom footsteps on the stairs. They told the Wylies how the din from the unseen noisemakers would sometimes become so loud the family could not hear the television. At these times, the sisters went to the staircase and demanded that the ghosts quit making noise. This usually quieted the ghosts.

Living with ghostly pranksters was an interesting part of childhood and adolescence for the sisters. Neither of them recalled anything frightening about their haunted home.

The Wylies realized that they must learn to share their home with the ghosts. Although the woman in the Rice

Planter's Room has not returned to rock her sick child, the playful ghosts of the second and third floors will still occasionally shake a bed or rattle down a hall. The Wylies and their guests find it impossible to ignore this ghostly teasing. But, because it is easy to live with, they are able to take it in stride.

The Pyatt House, built circa 1790,
is located at 630 Highmarket Street
on the corner of Screven Street.

Fyffe House

———— · · · ————

THE SPRING SEASON in Georgetown is always a magical interval between the clear crispness of winter and the shimmering heat of the coastal South Carolina summer.

Sometime during the middle of April, a few weeks after the spring equinox, the mass unfurling of thousands of patiently waiting buds surrounds Georgetown's historic homes in uncommon beauty.

The light-filled radiance of early spring daffodils and crocuses gives way to a dizzying profusion of vividly hued azaleas. The heady perfume of roses fills the warm, moist air.

Ancient, massive, live oak trees provide gracious trellises for twisting wisteria vines with delicate clusters of pale-purple flowers. Timeworn wrought-iron fences and pre-Revolutionary piazza railings are once again adorned with fragile vines bearing pale-yellow honeysuckle and deeper-saffron jessamine blossoms.

Bumblebees hum drowsily from bloom to bloom, assuring the grand unfurling from generation to generation.

For Pauline Moses, who had lived in the Fyffe House all her life, the spring of 1885 was more vividly green and headily fragrant than any spring she had ever known.

The reason for her appreciation of the splendors of this particular spring was her impending marriage.

Pauline's wedding, planned for early October of her twenty-first year, would be her family's first joyous event in several years.

Caroline, Pauline's mother, had passed away twelve years earlier. Since that time, Pauline's father Marcus was the sole parent for Pauline, her older sister Sarah, and her younger sisters Lily and Caroline.

In early December of the previous year, Marcus died, leaving the girls to mourn his loss.

However, both Marcus and Caroline were emigrants from Prussia, and they left their daughters an enduring legacy of dauntlessness and tenacity that enabled the young ladies to endure their unexpected bereavement.

The death of Marcus was an awful blow to Pauline, but the spring seemed to represent a rebirth of the hope and happiness she had lost during the winter. Part of Pauline's happiness came from the excitement she shared with her close friend Eliza Munnerlyn. Eliza was also engaged to be married in the fall.

During the year before he died, Marcus, a successful Georgetown merchant, had helped Pauline and Eliza collect trousseaus of the loveliest silks, satins, linens, and smooth cottons.

As the humid, warm spring days lengthened, Pauline and Eliza eagerly anticipated their weddings. The young women's enthusiasm turned to delight as they settled on an ingenious plan: they would marry on the same day, at the same hour.

The only problem with their plan was they could not attend each other's weddings. Pauline was to be married in an Orthodox Jewish ceremony, while Eliza's wedding would be in the Episcopalian church. Both weddings were scheduled for the eighth of October.

Throughout the hot, sultry summer, Pauline and Eliza spent many happy hours sitting on the long side piazza of the Moses home planning the intricate details of their weddings.

As Pauline's piazza faced the river and caught breezes cooled by the bay and the ocean, this was the most comfortable place for the girls to while away the hottest part of the day.

Built before the Revolutionary War, the Moses home, called the Fyffe House after its original owner, was well over a hundred years old in 1885. The house's serene smell of old wood blended with the deeper scent of gardenia blossoms from the bushes below the piazza, filling Pauline and Eliza's nostrils with summer aromas.

July passed, then August. These months were steamy and torrid, alleviated only by frequent afternoon thunderstorms.

It seemed to Pauline and Eliza that October would never arrive. The short distance between their houses seemed to lengthen in the humid heat, and the evening aggravation of biting mosquitoes caused the young ladies to limit their visits to daytime hours.

Finally October drew near. The end of September was very warm and humid, as was the beginning of October.

Mosquitoes were still rampant, and Pauline and Eliza hoped for a crisp, cool October eighth. They knew this kind of weather would make their wedding guests more comfortable, and banish most of the mosquitoes.

One morning during the first week of October, Pauline woke feeling extremely hot and damp. Her eyes hurt, too. She asked Lily to walk over to Eliza's home and explain that she was not feeling well and was going to spend the day resting in bed.

Perhaps, thought Pauline, the excitement of the approaching nuptials was physically overwhelming.

By the end of the day, Pauline was no better and Eliza

was also ill and feverish. The young women were much worse the following morning, and by evening it was obvious that both were desperately sick.

Their family doctors were summoned but could do nothing, for Pauline and Eliza had contracted the deadly yellow fever. Also known as hemorrhagic malaria, the disease was carried by mosquitoes.

By October seventh, both girls were dead.

They were buried on the day that they planned to be wed, the eighth of October. Pauline's funeral took place at nine in the morning. Eliza's was held in the early afternoon.

Pauline is buried behind the wrought-iron fence that surrounds Georgetown's old Hebrew cemetery. Eliza supposedly rests just across the street from Pauline, beyond the aged, red brick walls that enclose the churchyard of Prince George Winyah Episcopal Church.

In the years after the girls' death, strange laughter was heard emitting from the graveyards where the girls were buried. Many passersby would venture into the graveyards to look for the laughter's source, but, when they searched the grounds, no one could be found. Residents around Georgetown began to believe the mysterious voices laughing in the graveyard belonged to Pauline and Eliza.

Many seasons have passed since the spring and summer of Pauline and Eliza's great anticipation. Interred only a short distance apart, under the spreading, green-leaved branches of enormous old oak trees, the young ladies are still heard sharing the timeless delights of planning their wedding day, their girlish laughter echoing across the graveyards.

The Fyffe House, built circa 1770,
is located at 107 Cannon Street.

The Hebrew Cemetery, whose earliest graves
pre-date the Revolutionary War, is located
at 400 Broad Street at the corner of Duke Street.

The Prince George Winyah Episcopal Church
cemetery, which also pre-dates the
Revolutionary War, borders on Duke, Broad,
and Highmarket streets.

Cleland House

———— ∙ ∙ ∙ ————

ANOTHER TRAGIC wedding day left the ghost that now haunts the Cleland House. It is the ghost of a woman whose death was a terrible accident, conceived by no one and executed by what had appeared to be a beautiful and exquisite wedding gift.

Anne Withers lived with her parents on the Georgetown waterfront during the prosperous years preceding the Civil War. Her father was a socially prominent rice planter. Desiring to keep his family involved in Georgetown society, they lived most of the year in their Front Street townhouse.

Built in 1737, their comfortable home was reputed to be the oldest home in Georgetown. It was located near the point where St. James Street met the Sampit River.

The Cleland House originally faced the river. In 1730's Georgetown, Front Street was a secondary thoroughfare, so the rear of the home faced the road.

For thirty years, a chimney on each end of the house provided warmth against the cold winter and the perpetual dampness of the river. In 1767, one room was added at each end of the house, enclosing the chimneys.

The Cleland House already had a great deal of history behind it before it was occupied by the Withers family.

Many prominent guests had stayed in the home. During the Revolutionary War, Baron von Steuben and Baron deKalb were reputed to have been guests in the house while traveling with General Lafayette. Aaron Burr slept there preceding one of his visits to the Oaks Plantation where his daughter Theodosia lived. The Withers family was quite proud of the history of their house.

When Anne fell in love with a handsome sea captain, her father was a bit displeased but not very surprised. After all, the girl was raised beside the waterfront and she grew up intensely interested in the comings and goings of the tall-masted ships.

Anne's father hoped his pretty daughter would marry the son of another planter, but he had to admit that this sea captain was not bad at all. The fellow was quite wealthy, as well as being very handsome. He and Anne would have good-looking children.

Anne's parents, after being informed of the couple's desire to wed, gave their consent to the marriage. With their parents' blessings they went ahead with plans for the nuptials.

The wedding was scheduled to take place when the sea captain returned from his next voyage. The pair would marry downstairs in the Withers' home, with a reception in the ornate garden behind the Cleland House.

Anne was delighted but she prepared for her wedding with nervous anticipation. What if his ship was caught in a storm or stranded in the doldrums? What if he did not arrive for the wedding day?

The months flew by and, much to Anne's relief, her captain arrived in Georgetown, well and safe, a week before their wedding day.

One night, while catching his breath amidst the flurry of parties and social engagements that preceded the nuptials, the captain told Anne he had brought her a wedding present.

He reached in his pocket and brought out the gift, wrapped loosely in a linen handkerchief. As the material unfolded in his hand, a glittering gold bracelet appeared.

Anne gave an exclamation of delight and awe. In all her life she had never seen such a treasure.

The bracelet in her captain's hand was a chain of linked gold beetles. Each tiny creature had glistening gem eyes.

They were perfectly life-like, except for their gold countenance and lack of legs. Never, except in nature, had Anne seen beings of such flawless perfection. The beetles wrought in solid gold apparently had a foreign origin, for Anne had never seen insects quite like these around Georgetown.

As if he could read Anne's thoughts, her fiancé said, "It came from Egypt. The old trader I bought it from assured me it is a rare antiquity found in the tomb of an Egyptian princess."

As he struggled to undo the clasp to put the bracelet on Anne's wrist the captain went on, "No doubt it's very old and of rare quality, but I don't know about the Egyptian princess part. That sounds wonderfully mysterious, but the trader was a superstitious old sod, reeking of whiskey. He said he'd had nothing but bad luck since he bought this fine piece off a blind beggar."

When the clasp still would not come undone, and Anne finally withdrew her wrist. "Don't try anymore," she told her captain. "I won't wear it until our wedding. The clasp has probably not been worked in many years. My maid will get it open, even if she has to oil it and pry it loose."

When Anne returned to her room, she gave the bracelet to her maid and asked her to undo the clasp. She did not see the bracelet again until her wedding hour, several days later.

When the hour came for her to dress in her bridal finery, Anne found the bracelet laid along with all her other carefully chosen attire. When Anne was dressed, her maid gently fastened the glistening circlet of beetles around her wrist.

Anne turned her wrist this way and that, causing the bright stone eyes of the gold beetles to wink and glitter. What an extraordinarily lovely bracelet, she thought.

"It's time, Miss Anne," her maid advised the bride.

Anne stood up, gave her maid a hug, and walked out her bedroom door. The time had come to descend the stairs to the flower-festooned parlor where she would marry her captain. All her family and close friends were awaiting her descent.

Anne felt a tug of apprehension as she approached the staircase. This was such an important moment, the most serious, most happy moment of her life—and this bracelet was starting to itch, starting to prickle, starting to prick her . . .

Anne's maid heard a terrible scream tear from her mistress' throat. She dashed out of Anne's bedroom and into the upstairs hall to find Anne collapsed at the top of the stairs.

The bride was deathly pale in all her shimmering white finery. The only color on her ghostly alabaster form came from the gleaming red eyes of the golden beetles, and the blood that ran from the points where each beetle clung to her wrist.

Anne's maid tore at the bracelet as wedding guests ran up the stairs.

She gasped in horror as the bracelet finally gave way, the

previously hidden legs of the beetles now wrenched loose from her mistress' tender flesh. However, it was too late. Anne was already dead.

Anne's parents were overcome with shock and grief. Her fiancé could not forgive himself for giving his love such an unspeakably horrible present.

He immediately set sail for London, the bracelet locked away in a wooden box in his cabin.

The captain took the bracelet to the finest chemist in all London to have its structure and content analyzed. The chemist explained that the bracelet, perhaps never worn, was designed by the ancient Egyptians as a device to punish grave robbers. Each beetle had minute, sharp legs which held poison. These legs were hidden in the beetle body and ingeniously designed only to deploy when warmed by body heat.

After Anne had worn the bracelet for a short time, every needle-like leg came down and punctured the tender flesh of her wrist, poisoning her instantly.

Poor Anne died in terror, with no idea what was happening to her. She was only aware of the excruciating pain of thirteen fiery-eyed beetles digging into her wrist just as she was descending into the misty dream of her wedding.

Since that day, Anne has been seen many times in the garden behind her house. Some say the reason why Anne Withers occasionally comes back to her home by the river is the inexplicable terror of her death. She still does not understand what terrible force snatched her life away at its most joyous moment. Some nights, when the moon is nearly full and the river warms the cool breeze that blows in from the ocean, she can be seen in all her antebellum bridal finery walking through the back garden. And those who have seen her walking there will tell you that the look of bewilderment on her face reveals that she is wondering what went so horribly wrong on her wedding day long ago.

The Cleland House, built circa 1737,
is located at 405 Front Street
on the corner of James Street.

Morgan House

———— . . . ————

BY 1825, ARCHITECTURAL fashion changed drastically from the colonial styles of decades past.

Architectural features such as the beaded edges of clapboard exteriors, privacy doors leading onto piazzas, and nine-over-nine sash windows gave way to more austere and formal modes of the Federalist style.

The colonial law which required taxation based on street frontage was no longer in effect. Therefore, houses were built with their widest facades facing the street. In the case of a corner home like the Morgan House, the widest side faced the busiest street.

Main entrances were now built squarely in the center of the home and were entered directly from the street.

The builder of the Morgan House was a prosperous rice planter who already owned a large Black River plantation and another fine Georgetown townhouse.

He and his wife had raised their niece as their own child. When the time came for her to marry, they built an elegant two-and-one-half-story townhouse, designed in the modern, no-nonsense federalist style, as a part of her dowry.

The niece's new husband, Arthur Morgan, was a prosperous and enterprising Georgetown merchant. The home the planter built for the newlyweds came to be known as the Morgan House.

Mr. and Mrs. Morgan entertained often within the spacious first floor rooms of their elegant new townhouse.

The happy, prosperous years sped by, but soon the dark days of the Civil War arrived. Eventually, Union forces occupied the port of Georgetown, and the Morgans evacuated their townhouse because it was not safe for the family to stay in the city.

Union troops seized the Morgan House for use as a hospital for wounded troops. The poor soldiers who needed amputations or other surgery were operated on in the large, well-lighted dining room in the front corner of the house. The Morgans' huge, hardwood dining table served as an operating table. Many of those admitted to the makeshift hospital were seriously wounded and did not survive surgery in the dining room.

After the war, the Morgan family returned and resumed

life in their townhouse. Despite use as a hospital, the home had not been seriously damaged.

A few years after the war, Georgetown held a reunion for Confederate soldiers. This event took place directly across from the Morgan House, at the Winyah Indigo Society Hall on Prince Street. The reunion was a bittersweet celebration, for the Winyah Indigo Society began in the glorious, halcyon days of burgeoning wealth. It was started by a Santee Delta rice planter who wanted to create a fellowship of Georgetown County planters.

At that time, women were not allowed at meetings in the hall. The plantation masters cherished their male soirées as a time to discuss the latest news from London and indulge in "planter's punch." This punch was so strong that many had to tie themselves to their horses to travel safely back to their plantations.

The hall was also used as a political forum. Leading county residents often expressed their apprehensions and concerns at society gatherings in the years before the war.

Despite the disastrous outcome of the war, the reunion was a happy and resounding success. It lasted far into the night with speeches, delicious foods, and a joyous ball that rivaled antebellum festivities.

After the last waltz was finished, all the carriages had driven off, and the numerous out-of-town guests staying with the Morgans were fast asleep in their beds, a horrible din in the downstairs area of the Morgan House woke up the household. Terrible noises emitted from the dining room. The sounds of breaking glass, tumbling silverware, and heavy furniture screeching across hardwood floors rang through the otherwise quiet household. The din was punctuated by low-pitched moaning and groaning.

Mr. Morgan and his male guests rushed downstairs to capture the burglars, vandals, or whoever was creating such a row. When they reached the bottom of the stairs, they were amazed to find the dining room in perfect order.

Unable to find anything amiss or any explanation for all the strange noises, Morgan and the other guests went back to bed. After the full day and evening of festivities, they were too tired to stay up and ruminate over this early morning mystery.

In the light of the day, after everyone finished breakfast and a delicious cup or two of chicory-flavored coffee, the strange noises in the dining room became the subject of discussion.

No one in any of the neighboring homes heard anything unusual. The commotion the Morgans and their guests had experienced was confined to the Morgan House.

As the Morgans' guests bid their hosts farewell, all agreed that the night's noises were caused by the house settling. Still, deep in their hearts, everyone who heard the raucous commotion knew a house could not make those sounds unless it was falling down.

The Confederate celebration seemed to awaken the souls

of those suffering Union soldiers, and, once awakened, they did not go away. Over the years, the Morgans heard a loud racket coming from the dining room on many nights. The din and clamor always occurred after midnight and was always loud enough to awaken the entire household.

. . .

Over the next hundred years, subsequent owners of the Morgan House were also awakened by the noises.

Some of them had heard their home's history and were not entirely surprised when the late night clamor occurred. Others, with no knowledge of the curious dining-room phenomenon, dashed downstairs expecting to capture burglars the first time they heard the commotion. Of course, no one was there. No one, that is, except the ghosts of the Union soldiers who died during their surgery on the dining-room table.

The Morgan House, built circa 1825,
is located at 500 Prince Street
on the corner of Cannon Street.

Dupre House

———— · · · ————

IT IS DIFFICULT to picture a ghost in a newly renovated townhouse. This is why Mike, Roberta, and daughter Michelle found it difficult to believe that their recently acquired bed-and-breakfast inn had a ghost.

After purchasing the DuPre House, the family began renovations on the interior. During this extensive process, they were careful to preserve the exterior integrity of the circa 1790 structure as well.

During the renovation, an eighteenth-century-style privacy door was added. This heightened the colonial appearance of the inn's narrow, street frontage which was close to the sidewalk.

Approaching the DuPre House, guests of the inn can almost believe that they are stepping back into colonial days.

After entering the white-walled and blonde-wooded interior, the colonial atmosphere gives way to a sleek, modern ambiance. All is quiet, bright, airy, and serene.

The inn just doesn't seem ghostly.

The first indication of a ghostly presence came during the inn's renovation. During the heaviest part of construction, a young girl stopped by and told Mike, "You know, you have a little girl on the third floor, and she's trying to get out."

Mike politely dismissed the child and her odd comment. He was in the middle of a tremendous project that involved gutting the structure's interior and adding numerous bathrooms. He knew there was no way a child could enter the third floor without being noticed.

He gave the incident no more thought until months later when his wife was preparing a guest room on the third floor.

"Mommy, Mommy, Mommy," cried a small voice throughout the entire second floor. This prompted Roberta to go downstairs to find Mike. With all the guests gone for the day and her daughter Michelle in Florida, there was no one in the house who would call for a mommy. The couple was perplexed but never mentioned anything about the voice, a ghost, or a little girl to any of their guests.

Months after this incident, a guest on the second floor was unable to sleep. He took his newspaper into the bathroom to read so he wouldn't disturb his slumbering wife.

Something caught his eye over the edge of his paper. When he looked up, he saw a puff of smoke, rising from the tile floor. Upon closer examination, he found the floor was cool and no smoke was rising from its surface. He went back to his newspaper.

Then a second, larger puff of smoke appeared to rise from the floor. Again, the tiles were cool and the smoke dissipated almost instantly.

This was shortly followed by another puff of smoke, larger than the last.

This time, he was astounded to see a young child in the smoke.

The guest immediately folded his newspaper, stood up, turned off the bathroom light, went back into his room, and climbed back into bed beside his wife. He told Mike of the occurrence the next morning and asked him pointedly, "Do you have a ghost?" Mike was unable to give the man an answer, but he was beginning to suspect that he might indeed have a ghost.

Later, another guest asked if the inn had ever been on fire. The guest explained that she had smelled smoke in the house and later glimpsed the ghost of a woman wearing a long dress with an apron. When it became clear to her that there was no fire in the house, the guest had a strong impression that the woman and the smoke were related.

The third-floor, street-front bedroom is where the presence makes itself most pointedly known.

Mike and a guest made a startling discovery on a day when the third-floor rooms were unoccupied and undisturbed. Although no one had ventured near the third floor after the floors were carefully vacuumed, tiny footprints appeared in the smooth deep pile.

These footprints led across the room from the door to a blank wall. Each was in the perfect shape of a tiny foot. No prints led back across the room.

A short time later, after a guest's departure, Mike was making the bed in this same room. As he leaned over the right side of the bed, he suddenly felt the strong pressure of a hand bearing down on his right shoulder. No one was in the room with him, or even on the same floor.

Feeling a bit shaken, Mike temporarily abandoned the bedmaking and went downstairs.

Later he returned to the room to complete his task. While straightening the dust ruffle on the left side of the bed, Mike felt the same distinct and forceful pressure on his left shoulder. Again, no one was in the room or on the same floor.

The sunny, modern interior of the centuries-old DuPre House is home to something restless and intangible. What befell these people of the past that would cause their spirits to leave such lasting impressions?

Named after the DuPres, a French Huguenot family who owned the house before the American Revolution, the house had numerous owners before 1800.

Prior to the Civil War, the house was deeded to a Mrs. Easterling. Mrs. Easterling, a widow, operated Georgetown's lucrative ice house, which was left to her by her husband. During the year, except in the coldest part of winter, Mrs. Easterling's ice house had the only ice available in town. The ice was brought from the far north by ship, stored at the ice house, and sold to the townspeople.

Before her husband's death, Mrs. Easterling lived with him and their young child in the spacious Dupre House.

Although she continued to own the house after her husband's death, Mrs.Easterling and her child moved into an apartment above the business. As a widowed mother, this arrangement suited her better than living in her large house and walking back and forth to the ice house.

Late one hot summer afternoon, Mrs. Easterling was working in her office as her child played alone on the front steps of the ice house.

With childlike imagination and ingenuity, the little one had turned an old cigar box into a train. The homemade toy was brought to life by a candle that shone brightly through the cut-out windows.

When bedtime came, Mrs. Easterling's child left the box, with the candle still burning, on the steps.

During the night, Mrs. Easterling woke to find that her building was on fire.

She carried her child out of the flaming apartment and downstairs to the safety of the street. Then, leaving her child, she dashed back inside to save what valuables she could.

Mrs. Easterling underestimated the speed and severity of the blaze. While she was inside, the roof fell in, trapping her in the burning building. She perished in the flames.

Her child survived but, without parents, lived an unhappy childhood and eventually disappeared from Georgetown.

Is this why a small child and a woman linger about the upper stories of the Dupre House? Is it why many guests have seen smoke rising from the floor, seemingly out of nowhere? Mike, Roberta, and Michelle believe that the spirits of Mrs. Easterling and her child continue to haunt the Dupre House. They return to the house, where they knew happy times as a family, to escape the fire that killed one and destroyed the life of the other. Unfortunately, their escape from the fire is never complete. The smoke from the burning cigar box seems to forever follow the pair, eternally reminding them of their cruel fate.

Mike, Roberta and Michelle cannot say for certain that the spirits of Mrs. Easterling and her child inhabit their beautiful bed-and-breakfast inn. But the many strange encounters through the years have convinced them that ghosts do roam the Dupre House.

The Dupre House, built circa 1790,
is located at 921 Prince Street.